THE GOOLZ NEXT DOOR

THE MALLOW MARSH MONSTER

THE GOOLZ NEXT DOOR

BOOK 2

THE MALLOW MARSH MONSTER

GARY GHISLAIN

BOYDS MILLS PRESS
AN IMPRINT OF BOYDS MILLS & KANE
New York

Boyds Mills Press
An imprint of Boyds Mills & Kane, a division of Astra Publishing House
boydsmillspress.com
Printed in the United States of America

ISBN: 978-1-62979-678-9
eBook ISBN: 978-1-63592-397-1
Library of Congress Control Number: 2019950727

First edition
10 9 8 7 6 5 4 3 2 1

Design by Barbara Grzeslo
The text is set in Bembo.
The titles are set in Bourton Base Drop.

For Ilo, Sisko, and Elsa,
the monster squad inside my heart

"Sleep my baby,
Sleep, baby, do!
The Monster's coming
And he will take you.

Sleep my baby,
Sleep, baby, do!
The Monster's coming
And he will eat you."

Traditional Spanish Lullaby

1
WHAT'S
IN THE
BOX

"There's something strange about this foot." Frank Goolz poked it with the tip of a pencil.

"Yes," I agreed. "It's detached from its owner. That is pretty strange."

"Good point, Harold." He pushed away the cocoa and coffee cups and threw a dishcloth onto the kitchen table. Using the tip of his pencil and a teaspoon, he carefully removed the foot from the shoebox and set it on its side in the center of the towel.

Frank Goolz was a middle-aged man with salt-and-pepper hair in serious need of a comb or a cut. He was tall and slim and seemed to exist in his own world—except when the ghosties and ghoulies came knocking. As usual, he was wearing a white button-down shirt and black trousers. It was his preferred outfit for both monster-hunting and chillaxing at home.

Frank Goolz was also a famous author of best-selling horror novels about all manner of beasts: ghosts, zombies, mummies awakened by ancient curses . . . any nasty thing known to crawl the earth or swim the seas. His books were tomes of terror beloved by millions of readers around the world, including my mum and me.

Like everyone else, I had assumed these stories were birthed from the mind of a highly imaginative— and possibly batty—author of fiction. But since Frank Goolz and his two daughters had moved into the house next door, I had discovered the truth. His stories, even the most outlandish ones, weren't fiction at all. They were truthful accounts of his real-life investigations into the paranormal.

"Do you notice anything else?"

"Well . . . it stinks!" Ilona, his older daughter and the most amazing girl in the world, answered, covering her nose with her arm.

"Agreed," I said, and did the same with my own arm.

We were in the Goolz's kitchen and once again we were dealing with something gruesome. Just days before, we had solved a mystery involving a specter brought into being by an ancient artifact known as the Stone of the Dead. We had put the specter to rest and rescued the two boys it had kidnapped, and for about a nanosecond, life seemed to have gone back to normal. But then the Farrell twins showed up with a severed foot in a shoebox and asked Frank Goolz to help them find their missing mother. At present, they were standing hand in hand in the corner of the kitchen, watching us in a way that made my skin creep.

He looked up at them. "When did you say she disappeared?"

"She's been gone a week—"

"Almost two."

"And Dad's all alone—"

"Worrying."

"Moaning."

"Crying."

"All."

"The."

"Time!"

Ilona and I exchanged glances. I'd known the Farrell twins were . . . odd, but I'd never witnessed it. Until today, I'd mostly seen them from a distance. They were a couple of years younger than Ilona and me—maybe nine or ten—and identical from their tight brown

11

ponytails to their matching gray dresses, white tights, and leather lace-up boots. They looked like they had time-traveled from an era when people drove a horse and buggy and lit their homes with candlelight.

"We don't know if it's her foot—"

"For sure."

"Mom's foot is beautiful."

"Mom's beautiful."

"Do you think that's her foot?"

"For sure?"

"Hard to say." Frank Goolz scratched the stubble on his chin. "Ilo?"

Ilona's large brown eyes traveled from the foot to me and finally landed on the twins. She gave them a warm smile. "Let's hope not. Harold?"

"What?"

"Thoughts?"

I focused on the foot, trying to extract subtle clues that would impress her. The skin was greenish-gray, the toenails black. It stank madly and was swollen like a balloon about to burst.

"Well, I'm not a severed-foot expert. But that one's definitely . . . gross."

"Agreed."

Ilona Goolz and I were both seventh graders at Bay Harbor Middle School. We had become very fond of each other, which was a normal side effect of spending many nights together defeating a vengeful ghost and undoing an ancient curse. Also, we had kissed. Once. *Meaningfully.* So, I guess you could say we were kind of an item.

"Where did you say you found it?" Ilona asked the twins.

"In the marsh."

"By our house."

"In the water."

"We grabbed it—"

"With two sticks."

"It was very slimy."

"Yucky."

"Scummy."

They finished by speaking as one: "Did the Mallow Marsh Monster do that to our mom?"

"No way!" I told them.

I turned to Ilona. "The Mallow Marsh Monster doesn't exist. It's a kids' story."

She squinted at me. "Are we talking about some kind of swamp monster?"

"Yeah. Like a half-lizard, half-human thing. Fairy-tale stuff," I said, thinking she would join me in declaring that idea bonkers.

"Harold, swamp monsters are a thing," she said

instead. "Been there, done that." She nudged her dad. "Remember Carcassonne?"

"Sure thing, darling. The Carcassonne Creature nearly shredded me to pieces. What a beast!" He laughed, like it was nothing but a fond memory.

"I don't know about your carcass-thing," I told them.

"Car-cas-sonne," Ilona corrected me, pronouncing each syllable clearly. "It's a walled city in France."

"Well, I'm happy you guys have seen a real swamp monster while holidaying in France, but that's not the case here. The Mallow Marsh Monster isn't real. It's a silly local legend, like our own Bigfoot. But slimier."

"Interesting," Frank Goolz said thoughtfully, apparently ignoring the part about it not being real. "Why do you think the monster has anything to do with your missing mother?"

We all looked at the foot.

"Our parents say the monster comes out at night."

"To eat people—"

"And pets."

"And we live just by the Mallow Marsh."

"It's still not real," I insisted. "It's just a silly folk legend to scare kids."

"Tell him about the Carcassonne Creature!" Ilona's

little sister, Suzie, shouted from the hall. She was keeping her distance from the foot, staying close enough to listen in, but far enough away to keep from getting sick. Though she was easily the most intrepid of our outfit, Suzie couldn't stand the sight of blood or gore. Or severed rotten limbs, as we'd just discovered.

"We already did!" Ilona shouted back.

Suzie poked her head into the room and started telling me anyway. "It was a really giant, gooey creature, and it made an awful mess of its victims. Dad? Are we going after another Carcassonne Creature?" she added casually, as if she was asking what was for dinner.

Me: "No!"

Ilona: "Maybe."

Frank Goolz: "It seems likely."

"Cool." Suzie retreated to the hall. "A swamp monster will be a nice change after all those ghosts and poltergeists."

The Goolz sisters couldn't have been more different. Ilona was composed and focused, while Suzie was explosive and reckless. Ilona was tall and willowy and moved with a cool grace. Suzie was sturdy and compact and zigzagged through life, bumping into objects like an angry bee. Ilona had long, black hair that flowed in the wind. Suzie sported a short, blond, boyish mess.

Ilona always wore black dresses, a black coat, and black leather boots, while Suzie was all jeans, worn-out sweaters, and mismatched socks.

"Ilo, I think I'm going to barf!" she moaned from the hall. It must not have been a great idea for her to get closer to the foot and the stench emanating from it.

Ilona left the kitchen to comfort her sister. "You're going to be fine. Dad just needs to figure this thing out."

"We're almost done here, darling." Frank Goolz used two teaspoons to flip the foot upright. "Can you take a few pictures with your magic phone?" he asked me.

None of the Goolz had a cell phone, and Frank Goolz was fascinated by mine. He didn't seem to realize how commonplace they were.

I took my phone out of the kangaroo pocket of my hoodie and snapped a few pictures of the foot. On screen, it looked even nastier. "Maybe I should use the flash," I said. I turned on the flash and took another set of pictures. The result was even more dreadful.

"Wait a second. Did you see that?" Frank Goolz leaned so close to the foot that his nose almost touched it. "Can you use that light on your phone?"

I switched on the flashlight and held it over the foot.

"Amazing!" he said, snatching the phone from me. He moved it as close as possible to the sharp cut above the ankle and used his other hand to press the eraser side of the pencil against the graying flesh. He pushed the pencil into the middle of the cut. "That's why this foot looks so odd. It's just skin and flesh." The pencil slipped deeper inside. My stomach turned, but Frank Goolz looked entranced.

"The bones are gone," he said.

"Gone where?" I asked.

"Exactly!" He dropped my phone on the table and turned to the twins. "What were you doing in the marsh anyway?"

"Catching snakes."

"We catch them for our parents."

"Dad's a doctor."

"And Mom's a biologist."

"They study them—"

"*All. The. Time!*" they finished together, then rolled their eyes in synchronized loops.

I hadn't known that their parents were scientists, though they did look the part: discreet, bespectacled, and unfashionable, with a touch of nerdy *je ne sais quoi*.

I switched off the light on my phone. "Could a doctor or a scientist remove bones from a foot?"

"Impossible." Frank Goolz grabbed an empty cup and rolled it over the toes. They were as soft as an empty plastic glove. "Even a skilled surgeon couldn't do it without damaging it noticeably." He kept pressing the toes with the cup. "See? No scars, no cuts. This is unbelievable."

"Can you help us?" the twins asked.

"Yes," Ilona said firmly from the kitchen doorway. "We're going to help you find your mother."

She turned to her father. "Are you going to contact your new best friend, Officer Miller?"

Officer Miller was the police officer who had interrogated us when we found a dead man in a crab tank. He had a good sense of humor, but he'd definitely wonder why a famous writer, his two daughters, and a boy in a wheelchair had gotten mixed up in another unexplainable, possibly criminal conundrum.

"This foot defies the laws of science and reality. Officer Miller couldn't handle it. This is definitely *our* kind of thing." He gestured with the teaspoon at himself, me, and Ilona. "And Suzie too," he added when she harrumphed loudly.

"Darn straight!" Suzie called from the other room. I felt a pang of pride at the idea that they saw me as a permanent member of their team.

"Dad doesn't want us to go to the police, anyway," one of the twins said.

"Why?" Ilona asked.

"He doesn't trust them."

"Or the hospital."

"Or anybody in Bay Harbor."

"Or television."

"Or the *gov-ern-ment*."

"Or anything that comes from Newton."

Newton was the closest place to Bay Harbor that you could call a city. It's where you could find the police precinct, hospital, and mall, and—unlike Bay Harbor—it had more people than seagulls.

"Your father sounds like a very wise man," Frank Goolz said. He used the pencil to push the foot back onto its side. "Let's go talk to him. I just need to do one more thing while the rest of you get ready to go."

"What are you going to do?" I asked.

"Just trust me." He shooed us out of the kitchen and closed the door behind us.

"What do you think he's doing?" I asked Ilona as I grabbed my jacket from one of the many unopened crates scattered around the hall. I wondered if the Goolz would ever unpack.

"No idea." Ilona picked up a pair of sneakers and

19

handed them to her sister. "We're going out," she told her. "Can you handle it?"

Suzie nodded feebly. She dropped from the crate to the floor to put on her shoes, but then she just stayed there, staring at them helplessly.

"You'll feel better as soon as you get some fresh air," Ilona said, bending to help her.

A loud *THUD* came from the kitchen.

The twins had been standing by the door, quietly watching us.

"What is he doing to our foot?"

"It sounds like he's hammering it."

"Bouncing it."

"Slapping it."

"He's not going to destroy it—"

"Is he?"

"Don't worry. There's always a good reason for everything he does, no matter how mad it seems," I said. I went out to the front porch to wait for them.

Mum was in our yard, weeding the garden. I waved and she waved back.

At first, Mum had been thrilled that a famous writer like Frank Goolz had moved in next door. But she soon realized that he was way weird and that his daughters were troublemakers who wouldn't hesitate to drag me

20

into all sorts of danger. After fetching me from the police station at the end of our first adventure, she'd imposed a complete embargo. I was to stay away from the Goolz. Forever. Earlier today she'd lifted it partially, and I was now allowed to spend time with them as long as I stayed on our property or theirs.

"You're coming home already?" Mum dropped a handful of weeds in her wicker basket.

"Oh, no, not yet," I said, looking back into the Goolz's home. I saw Frank Goolz coming out of the kitchen, carrying the shoebox. The sugary stink of the rotten foot followed him. "Just coming out to say hello. Hello!"

"Hello." Mum frowned and tilted her head, waiting for a better explanation.

I waved awkwardly and flipped my chair around. I went back in the house and closed the door. Ilona had finished lacing her sister's sneakers and was stepping into her own leather boots. She put on her black coat and added a black beret. She looked very European, a little mysterious, and terribly pretty.

"We're using the back door," I said, already heading that way.

"Why?" Frank Goolz threw on a black coat and stepped his bare feet into black leather boots.

"There's no way Mum will let me leave with you guys."

Last time I followed the Goolz past their front gate, I ended up on the wrong side of a shotgun. Mum wasn't pleased at all.

I went out the back door and stopped at the top of the steep porch stairs.

"I need to build another ramp," Frank Goolz said. He had already built one leading to their front porch, but none of us had anticipated needing a second exit to escape undetected.

"You sure do, Dad." Ilona grabbed the handles of my wheelchair and gave me the nicest smile. "I have a feeling this is going to be a regular occurrence."

Her dad grabbed the front of my chair to help carry me down. The twins stood at the threshold and watched, probably wondering why we needed to sneak around.

"We're weird," Suzie told them. "Don't worry about it." They followed her down the stairs.

"Mum would literally kill us!" I said as they gently set my chair on the muddy ground. I grabbed my wheels and shot for the back alley, smiling inside at the thought of another adventure with the Goolz.

"She's such a wonderful woman, your mother,"

Frank Goolz said, walking at his usual quick pace beside me. "So strong-minded."

I turned into the alley, checking over my shoulder to make sure we were all blocked from view by the Goolz's house. I couldn't see Mum, which meant she couldn't see us. We could make it all the way to Newton without her suspecting a thing.

2

DOCTOR
SUPER
STRANGE

"No one ever visits us."

"Dad has no friends."

"No parents."

"*No-bo-dy!*"

"Mom used to have friends."

"They're not welcome in our house anymore."

"Mom says they're *blab-ber-ers*."

"That means they can't keep a secret."

The twins stopped in the middle of the road and pointed toward the marsh. "That's our house!"

I could already see the roof of their house rising above the thick screen of high grass. It was a rotting old building right at the edge of the marsh, the very last house you saw before leaving Bay Harbor on the road to Newton. Each time Mum and I drove past it, I couldn't help wondering how anyone could live in such a gloomy, rundown place.

"I thought that place was abandoned," Suzie said.

The Farrells' house might have been dark red in the past, like most wooden houses in our town, but the red paint had dulled into a sickly brown, and the base of the building was covered in pale-green moss. The land was slowly being swallowed by weeds and water creeping over from the marsh.

"Dad's going to be surprised to see you."

"We didn't tell him where we were going."

"He thinks we're in the marsh."

"Looking for more snakes."

They resumed walking toward their house and we followed them.

"Did you see their eyes?" Ilona asked me.

The twins looked back at us. "We were born like this."

"Ruth has one brown eye and one green."

"Beth's eyes are both brown."

"That's cool. It's a good way to tell you apart," I said.

Their three brown eyes and one green lingered on me.

"Were you born like that?"

"We were born different, too."

"Mom says we're special."

"She means it in a really nice way."

"Mom is really nice."

"Is yours nice, too?"

They were like the Goolz girls. They didn't pretend not to notice that I used a wheelchair. And they were definitely not shy about bringing it up.

"My mum's nice. And I wasn't born like this. I climbed on a chair to reach for a plum on a high branch. The chair broke. I fell on my back. It was eons ago."

"He doesn't even like plums," Ilona said, stealing my punchline.

The twins stopped again as we reached a path leading from the road to their house.

"We don't like plums either."

"They're tart."

"We like apples."

"Do you like apple pie?"

"Mom makes delicious apple pies."

"When she's not working on snakes."

"Apple pies are nice," Suzie said, stepping close to a sign she'd noticed by the mouth of the path. She pushed some high grass aside to read it. "*Danger. Quicksand. Stay Away.*" She grinned. "Great!"

The marsh had nearly digested both the sign and the path in a mixture of green moss and black fungus.

Frank Goolz squeezed my shoulder and followed the twins and Suzie. "Perfect setting for a horror story. Wouldn't you say, Harold?"

The unbearable odor of the shoebox that he carried under his arm confirmed we weren't on our way to a picnic.

Ilona and I stayed on the road as they walked up the path and disappeared from view. We hadn't been alone for the longest time. Between the ghost hunt and Mum's embargo, we hadn't had a chance to do anything normal together—like talking, joking, going to the boardwalk, studying, or anything else that didn't involve supernatural creatures or severed limbs.

"You all right?" she asked.

I shrugged. "Sure."

"Should we follow them before they solve the foot mystery without us?"

"You got it."

We reached the path. The muddy, trampled ground was boss-level difficult to maneuver with my chair. Ilona walked a few feet ahead of me, kicking stones and sticks out of my way.

She stopped to pick up a big piece of rotten wood

that blocked the path. She smiled and I smiled back. I loved when she did things like this. Helping me without making anything of it. Like we were meant to explore the world together in perfect harmony.

"Oh, bananas. They're at it again," I heard Suzie say from the high grass ahead. "They're stupid in love, just so you know," she clarified for the twins.

Ilona rolled her eyes. I slapped my forehead. "Your sister's nuts." I tried to laugh it off, but it came out as a tense chuckle.

Ilona threw the piece of wood aside, and it splashed into some water, out of sight. She brushed the mud off her hands, and we kept going up the path, both of us redder than begonias in spring.

We came to what looked like a dead end of weeds. But the twins and Suzie had already disappeared beyond it. Frank Goolz must have been waiting for us because his arm came back through the grass and he and Ilona made an entryway for me. They stood on either side like ushers holding a curtain.

"See you on the other side." I gave them a silly military salute and crossed through to the strange world of the Mallow Marsh.

A dark brown shape appeared ahead. Once I got a little closer, I realized it was a rusted old pickup truck that must have been rotting there for a long time. The tires were flat and half sunk in mud. Like the sign and the path, the marsh had almost completely absorbed it.

"This one's never getting out," Ilona said, coming out of the grass behind me and knocking on the rusty door.

Looking past her, I noticed a network of ancient boards that started at the edge of the Farrells' yard and led up to, around, and even through the marsh. "Look," I said. "It's a dock—or it used to be. I never saw it before."

"A world hidden from ours. I like it," Frank Goolz said. He squashed a mosquito on his neck and we continued toward the house.

The twins ran in, shouting for their dad and leaving the door wide open behind them.

Suzie followed them in. "It smells really weird in here!" she called back to the rest of us.

When I entered, the chemical stench made me gasp. "Suzie's right. It stinks!"

Frank Goolz inhaled noisily through his nose. "Formalin," he said.

As my eyes adjusted to the dim light, I saw that the hallway was lined with shelves, from floor to ceiling. But instead of books and family photos, they were full of mason jars. "Holy cheese! That's a lot of dead creatures," I said as I peered through the cloudy glass of the closest one.

"Now we know what they're doing with all those snakes they catch in the marsh," Ilona said, coming up beside me.

"It's not only snakes." Suzie moved from one jar to the next. "Here's a mouse. That's a lizard. And . . . is that a brain?"

Frank Goolz tapped the jar she was pointing at. "Correct, darling. That's a brain. It could have belonged to a cat. Or a small dog, maybe."

I moved closer to the brain. It was both disturbing and irresistible. "What kind of crazy person collects cat brains?"

"It's a beaver's brain," someone mumbled behind us. We turned around as Ed Farrell came out of the basement. "It died of rabies. It's quite rare that they get infected with it."

He stood in the doorway and used his rubber-gloved hands to brace himself on the frame. Even his thick-rimmed glasses couldn't hide the plump, dark pockets under his eyes.

Mr. Farrell took a couple steps toward us, his gloves leaving thick red smudges on the doorframe.

His lab coat was spattered in red too.

I looked at Ilona. *Blood!* I mouthed. She nodded back at me.

The twins came out of the basement behind him.

"Dad's sleepy—"

"And dirty."

"And a little smelly."

"He hasn't slept—"

"For days!"

He was about the same age as Frank Goolz, somewhere in his forties. His thick black hair was slicked back, though a few greasy locks had escaped and stood straight up. He was well overdue for a shave, a change of clothes, and—by the smell of it—a shower.

"Hello there, sir." Frank Goolz held out his hand, ignoring the bloodied medical gloves.

"Oh. The famous writer," Farrell responded softly. He removed a glove and shook Frank Goolz's hand oddly, holding it way too long, like this basic human interaction was unfamiliar to him.

"I love your novels. Especially the one with the mad alchemist." Farrell finally let go of Frank Goolz's hand. Then he scratched his head, freeing more locks of hair, which sprang up to join the others. He gazed at the ceiling, falling silent for several long moments. Then he seemed to reboot his mind and said, "You could sign it if I can find it, but it might have gotten lost."

"We move a lot."

"We go from one place—"

"To the next."

"*All. The. Time!*"

"I didn't come to sign books." Frank Goolz looked at both sides of his hand, probably checking if Ed Farrell had gotten blood on him.

Mr. Farrell removed his other glove, and the smile dropped from his face. "Why are you here exactly?" he asked as if the thought had just occurred to him.

"Your daughters asked for our help," Ilona said.

"Help with what?"

I made a mental note to tell the Goolz that Ed Farrell had fresh bruises and scratches on his neck, like something had tried to strangle him.

"They want us to find their mother."

I knew I was biased when it came to Ilona, but I couldn't help admiring how composed and fierce she looked while talking to this strange man.

"Their mother is fine," he said, and then seemed to realize we were all looking at the blood on his lab coat. He shook his head and walked away, abandoning us and his daughters in the hall.

"I guess we should follow him," Frank Goolz suggested, and we did.

Farrell went straight for the kitchen sink, where he dropped his gloves on top of a pile of dirty dishes.

"Mr. Farrell, can you tell us where your wife is?" Frank Goolz asked.

Farrell took off his lab coat and threw it on the counter. "She's . . ." he turned on the faucet and started washing his hands with steaming water. "Gone."

Their kitchen was like the rest of their house—messy and old and odd. The floor was covered with ancient greenish linoleum that had come unglued at the corners and been repaired with duct tape here and there. The appliances looked like they belonged in a museum and the yellowy-white fridge was purring noisily.

"Gone where?" Ilona asked.

"South?" Farrell said.

He dried his hands on an unbloodied corner of the lab coat and turned to us. His graying white shirt was drenched at the armpits and, though he'd been home alone, he wore a black tie, which hung loose around his neck. His breast pocket held a jumble of pens that had leaked spots of blue, red, and black ink into the dingy fabric. His glasses were fogged with steam. Altogether, he was a picture-perfect representation of a mad scientist who had spent many sleepless nights waiting for a thunderstorm to reanimate the dead.

"Well!" Frank Goolz said cheerfully. He took the shoebox from under his arm and lifted the lid. "Do you recognize this?" He extended his arms to show Mr. Farrell the contents of the box.

Mr. Farrell took off his glasses and blinked at the foot. He didn't register any shock or horror, nor did he appear disturbed by the unbearable smell. "Oh," he whispered. He cleaned his glasses with the unbuttoned bottom of his shirt, then pushed them back onto his nose. "Where did you find it?"

"Your daughters found it in the marsh," I said.

He turned to me and squinted like he had just noticed my presence.

"We told them."

"About Mom."

"That's she's gone."

"And that you're worrying—"

"Or crying."

They looked at each other.

"*Sometimes*," they finished carefully.

"Nonsense! I'm not worrying. Mom's fine, absolutely fine. She will be back very soon," he told them, then nodded toward the foot. "And this foot is mine."

34

I instinctively looked down at his feet. They were both definitely there, secured in soft black shoes over dingy white tennis socks.

Frank Goolz put the lid back on. "Do you collect severed limbs?" he asked politely.

"It came from the morgue," he said. "My wife and I need it for our research. It should be in our freezer down in the lab." He looked down at his daughters. "Did you take it from there and make up a story for Mr. Goolz?"

"No!"

They pointed at the marsh.

"It was out there."

"In the water."

"All slimy."

"And yucky."

"We're not lying!"

"It's okay, girls. I'm not angry."

I was watching Ilona, who was watching Mr. Farrell even more intensely than her dad was. "Can we speak with your wife, Mr. Farrell?" she asked pointedly. "On the phone, I mean? We'd like to make sure she's fine."

"I told you she's fine!" he snapped. "That should be enough!"

We looked at him silently for an awkwardly long

time. Frank Goolz slapped another mosquito on his neck.

"I'm sorry," Ed Farrell said, composing himself. He cleared his throat and forced a smile. "I'm going to need my foot back."

Ilona turned to her dad and gave her head a minute shake.

"I'm sure you do," Frank Goolz said, but he didn't hand over the box. He snapped his fingers like he had just remembered something. "About this foot."

"What?"

"All the bones have been removed, but the foot is completely intact. It's quite extraordinary. Do you know how it could be done?"

"That is . . . part of our research," Farrell said hesitantly. But the surprise in his eyes told a different story. "I need to return to my work, if you don't mind."

He reached for the box. Frank Goolz took a step back. "What exactly is your research about?"

"Rare infections."

"Like a bone-dissolving infection?"

Mr. Farrell's face lit up. "Yes! That's about right." He reached for the box again and this time Frank Goolz let him have it.

Mr. Farrell set it on the counter on top of his bloody

lab coat. "I hate to come across as unfriendly. But I have so much work and so little time."

"But Dad—" the twins started, but their father cut them off.

"We'll entertain our new friends another time when I am less busy." He shooed us out of the kitchen and walked us to the front door. "You people have a nice day." And he shut the door without another word.

We stopped when we reached the wrecked pickup truck.

I looked back at the strange house. "Did you see the bruises on his neck? And all that blood!"

"You shouldn't have given him the foot," Ilona told her dad. "That might be all that's left of Mrs. Farrell."

Frank Goolz smiled and put his hand on her shoulder. "I didn't give him all of it. I cut a nice slice of it before we left the house. It's in our freezer at home if we ever need to have it analyzed."

"You cut off a slice of the foot?" Suzie yelled. "Like it was ham?"

"That's disgusting!" I said, smiling because I thought it was genius, too.

Suzie inspected the inside of the truck through the grimy passenger-side window, then opened the door.

A cloud of fetid odor wafted out. "Everything stinks today!"

She took a step back, waving her hands and arms, trying to dissipate the stench.

I was the closest to the open door and the first to take a look inside the cab. "Guys!"

They gathered around me. We leaned together inside.

"Oh, cheese!" Ilona said.

The entire interior, from the dashboard to the fake leather seats, was covered in deep gouges with patterns of three or four lines, like someone—or *something*—had tried to claw its way out.

"What's that?" Suzie hunkered down, picking up what looked like a bunch of white pebbles scattered on the passenger seat. She held them out on the palm of her hand.

Frank Goolz pinched one between his fingers. "Teeth. Human."

"What kind of crazy dentist did that?" I picked one up and examined it just like he had, even though my stomach roiled with disgust.

"Not the type that gives you a toy once he's done," Suzie said, giving all the teeth to her dad. I gave him the one I held quickly, then brushed my hand off on the front of my hoodie.

Frank Goolz held the teeth loosely in his fist, rattling them like dice before dropping them into his coat pocket. "This is getting more interesting by the minute."

I looked back into the cab. My eyes traveled from one set of scratches to the next. Some of the scratches were lighter than the others and didn't follow the same pattern. "Wait. These right here aren't random."

I took out my phone and switched on the flashlight.

"You're right, Harold. It's a message," Ilona said.

I brought the light very close to the dashboard. Someone had clumsily carved a few nearly invisible words.

"*I'll be back for you,*" Ilona read. I quickly looked up at the Farrell's house.

The twins were observing us through one of the windows. They waved in perfect synchronicity—and I shivered.

3

LIFE
IS
CAKE

We reentered the Goolz's home by the back door and exited out the front like we had never left.

"No need to rush, Harold," Ilona said, trotting beside me. "I'm sure she doesn't know a thing."

Mum wasn't in her garden anymore, and I was silently praying that she hadn't come over to check on me while we were away.

She stepped out to the porch as the girls and I were crossing the little bridge running between our two properties. She looked terribly concerned, which concerned me terribly.

She cleared her throat loudly, and I braced myself for a storm.

"Would you like to come in for tea?" she asked the

Goolz. I sighed, thanking all my angels.

"Told ya," Ilona whispered, smiling at me. "She's in the dark. Mission Escape is a success."

"I baked a cake," Mum said gravely. She made it sound like a tragedy. "I'd love for you to join us."

"Wonderful!" Frank Goolz shouted from his porch. "We love cake!" He zoomed toward our house, oblivious to Mum's pained face and tense posture.

"It's a cheesecake," Mum clarified, forcing an awkward smile.

I could already smell the delicious, warm, welcoming aroma wafting out the front door.

"Was that the Farrell twins I saw going into your house?" she asked as we joined her on the porch. "Do you know them?"

"Not really," Frank Goolz answered, unzipping his leather boots. Mum watched him kick them off and walk through the door like he owned the place.

"Oh, yes, well, make yourself at home," she said in an artificially light tone.

I glanced at Ilona and tried to telepathically ask her to get her dad under control before he ruined Mum's desperate attempt at reconciliation.

"They're really interesting girls," Suzie said, eyeing the enormous cheesecake cooling by the kitchen window. "They do all kinds of super-fun stuff—like catching snakes in the marsh and storing them in jars once they're dead!"

Mum looked alarmed, but apparently chose not to comment. "Why did they come to see you?" she said instead, transferring the cake from the counter to the table.

"They wanted to meet a famous writer, that's all," I said, deciding I was the most qualified to lie to Mum. "They're a little different."

"How so?"

"They're two but they're really one. Like they speak as one. They move as one," Ilona explained. "They're very . . . synchronized."

"Interesting. I didn't see them leave. I thought they were still in there with you." Mum put a sharp knife beside the cake on the table.

"They left out the back," Frank Goolz said, pulling out a chair.

"Oh."

I could feel another dozen dangerous questions bubbling up in Mum's mind.

"Yeah, a little different, like I said," I said loudly, trying to distract Mum from thinking too much about the Goolz's back door.

"They're not different at all!" Suzie sat down at the table, right in front of the cake. "They're super nice. I really like them. And I love cheesecake," she added pointedly.

"I'm sorry we came empty-handed." Frank Goolz winked at me. "No sweets. No flowers. Not even a severed foot!" And he laughed.

Mum was at the sink, filling the kettle, which gave Ilona a chance to sit by her dad and elbow him hard on the arm.

"A severed foot?" Mum said with an awkward fake laugh. "You have the strangest sense of humor."

"Yeah, Dad's funny like that." Ilona smiled innocently as Mum came back to the table and started laying out plates, cups, glasses, forks, spoons, a teapot, and a pitcher of homemade lemonade.

"Well," Mum said, looking around uncomfortably. "I know we got off to a rough start." She was referring to the Goolz dragging me off on an adventure that had me nearly mauled by dogs, shot by a criminal, and ending face-to-face with a murderous ghost—not that she knew anything about that last part. "I would like to put that in the past and begin by saying that I'm sorry I called you all those bad names."

"What names?" he asked.

"Well." She cleared her throat again. "Irresponsible. Reckless. Inconsiderate."

"Didn't you call him *nuts* a couple times too?" Suzie added, looking at me for confirmation.

"I regret those words. I really do. They were insensitive. I was just . . . so worried about Harold."

"No worries, Margaret." Frank Goolz leaned over to tap my shoulder. "Harold's safe with us now. Right, buddy?"

"Totally!" Ilona and I said at the same time.

"You guys sound just like the twins!" Suzie scoffed.

Mum sighed deeply. I could tell that she had rehearsed this speech while baking her cake. "Can we put all those bad feelings behind us and start anew?"

"Sure," Frank Goolz said simply, offering her his best smile.

"Good." She picked up the knife. "I would also like to thank you for building the ramp for Harold. It was a very considerate thing to do and it meant a great deal to him. And to me. So . . . thank you, Frank. And you are not . . . *nuts*. I'm sorry I said that."

"Okay. Enough with the speech. Cake!" Suzie grabbed a plate and extended half her body over the table to be the first served. "I'd like a really huge slice."

"Building the ramp was a natural thing to do," Frank

Goolz told her. "Harold is one of us. We realized today that I need to build another one out the back."

Ilona kicked his leg under the table, but Mum didn't seem to notice anything suspicious. I think her mind had stopped registering anything after he said that I was one of them. "That's very kind of you." She rewarded him with an even larger slice than the one she had given Suzie.

We all ate silently for a while. I kept looking at Mum. Inviting the Goolz, offering neighborly peace, and thanking him hadn't been easy for her. She was slowly recovering and breathed more calmly with each sip of tea. Soon, she managed to return to small talk.

"So, Frank, Harold told me you used to come here a long time ago, when you were a student."

Suzie stopped wolfing down her slice of cake. "We don't talk about that!" She pointed her fork at Mum. "Ever."

Mum's eyes opened wide. Her discomfort with the Goolz returned in a flash. "I'm sorry," she blurted and cut another slice of cake. "I didn't mean to pry. More cake?" Her voice could climb to a really high pitch when she was nervous.

"Dad doesn't like to talk about the time before we were born. When it was just him and our mom,"

Ilona explained more smoothly than her sister.

"Exactly!" Suzie kept pointing her fork at Mum. "And yes, I will have more cake."

"Though, it's true," Frank Goolz said. "I used to come here with my wife before we were married." He took a bite of cake and we all watched him chew thoughtfully.

"We used to spend entire summers here, Nathalie and I," he finally continued. "She loved Bay Harbor."

Suzie put down her fork. "Mom loved it here?" she asked softly.

"Very much."

I checked on Ilona. She had also stopped eating her cake and had all her attention on her dad. "What did she love about it?" she asked eagerly.

"Everything. It was her favorite place in the world." He was the only one still eating. "She always thought we would end up living here. She loved your house, actually." He smiled at Mum. "She would always point it out when we took walks on the beach. She'd say that someday, this house . . . your house . . . would be ours and we would live in it happily ever after."

He stopped talking. He had finished his cake. There was nothing but the sound of the ocean for a moment. And then a passing seagull called us back to the present.

"I'm sorry, I didn't mean to bring back painful memories," Mum said.

"No, that's fine. They're nice memories." He sat back, picking up his cup of tea. "When I decided to move here with the girls, I inquired about your house. I was told it wasn't for sale. Luckily, the one next door was. Close enough."

I turned to look at their house through the kitchen window. "So, it's not totally random that we're neighbors?"

"It's not random at all, Harold. It was set in motion a long time ago."

"It sounds like destiny," Ilona said.

"It doesn't only *sound* like destiny. That's precisely what it is," Frank Goolz said.

Ilona and I looked at each other. Then, in perfect synchronicity, we got to work on our slices of cake.

Suzie picked up her fork again and pointed it at me this time. "You're living in our house, Harold!" She took another large bite of cake. "But that's okay," she said with her mouth full. "I prefer ours. You can stay in this one."

"I'm happy that Nathalie's favorite house is owned by absolutely wonderful people." Frank Goolz finished his tea in two gulps. "Margaret?"

"Yes?"

"Could I get another piece?"

"Of course!" She sliced it eagerly.

. . .

After we finished our cake, we went out to the porch with our lemonade and tea to watch the sun disappear behind the hills, which was Mum's favorite activity besides gardening.

Everybody was more relaxed, including Mum. Her idea to make peace over cake seemed to have mostly been a success with just a few hiccups, like Suzie menacing her with a fork and yelling at her. And with people like the Goolz, that was more or less acceptable weirdness.

The Goolz were sitting on the swing, Mum was rocking in the rocking chair, and I was by her side. We were all waiting silently for the magical moment when the sky over the sea turned from orange to red. Frank Goolz looked particularly absorbed, and I wondered if he was still lost in memories of his late wife.

He looked away from the ocean and turned to Mum. "Do you know much about the Mallow Marsh Monster?"

Frank Goolz wasn't reminiscing about his youth after all. He was doing his usual thing: thinking about monsters.

"Oh, sure." She poured them both more tea. "It's a local folk story. Everybody here loves talking about the Marsh Monster."

"Do you think it has something to do with the foot?" Suzie asked her dad.

I widened my eyes at Suzie and Ilona whispered a few harsh words in what sounded like German.

"What foot?" Mum asked, picking up on the secretive vibes. "You already mentioned a severed foot."

"It's something for his next book. It's going to be a . . . a severed foot story. Right, Dad?" Ilona said quickly.

"Absolutely. And I believe it's going to be a Mallow Marsh Monster story too."

"What's the monster like?" Suzie put down her lemonade and pushed her feet against the coffee table, gently rocking the swing. "Is it like a giant tortoise with a lion head that gobbles people up and spits out their body parts, minus the bones?"

Mum laughed and put down her cup. "No, it's nothing like that. It's like a part-human, part-reptile, part-abominable creature that goes around the marsh looking for victims. You can see some old sketches of it at the Heritage Museum here in town." She tightened the plaid blanket she had thrown over her shoulders and shivered. "Thank God such a creature could only exist in one of your scary books."

Ilona and I looked at each other.

"Yes. Thank God for that," Ilona said dryly.

I took out my phone and Googled the monster. The search took me directly to the Bay Harbor Heritage Museum webpage.

"There." I clicked on a picture and showed them the screen.

It was an old black-and-white photo of a group of Bay Harbor men posing with guns in front of the marsh. All of them had thick mustaches or beards and looked very stern and maybe a little sad.

"Who are those people?" Suzie snatched the phone from me to see the picture better. "Can you find a real picture of the monster?"

"There won't be a *real* picture of it." Mum took the phone from her and looked at the hunters. "You can't photograph a legend."

"I can show you some good pictures of the giant tortoise with the lion head. And that was supposed to be a legend too. Only it was in France so they call it *le horrible monstre ooh la la*," Suzie said with a perfect French accent.

Mum gave me my phone back, and I scrolled

50

through more pictures. I stopped on a drawing of the monster. It was a horrific humanoid creature with balloon-like red eyes and green skin covered in scales. Its gaping jaws were full of pointed teeth, and its claws looked like long dark knives. In the drawing, it was attacking a group of people, biting one in the neck while the others ran away, arms up in the air. I handed the phone to the Goolz.

"That thing doesn't look like the Carcassonne Creature at all," Suzie said, sounding disappointed. "Have you ever dealt with a creature like this one?" she asked her dad. "I mean in one of your books," she added reluctantly when Ilona kicked her.

"Not until now."

"That is such a good idea for your next book. Monster stories are fun." Mum took the phone back to look at the picture. "Oh. This one doesn't look so fun. You're going to terrify your readers. Look at those teeth!"

She looked away from the phone and back at the ocean. The last glow was fading, and suddenly it was dark. "Should we call it a night?" She gave me the phone, threw back the plaid blanket, and stood up. "Tomorrow is a school day."

I tapped the picture on the screen. It linked to a

Wikipedia page about the Mallow Marsh Monster. I didn't want the Goolz to leave. "Mum? Can we invite them for dinner?"

She gave me a surprised look. She had already thrown an impromptu cake party that had been emotionally exhausting for her, and now I was pushing it even further.

"We never have guests. Please, Mum."

"I guess I could whip up something simple," she said hesitantly. She picked up some of the glasses and the teapot. I knew she hated to be forced into things, but I knew she wouldn't want to be rude either. "Well, only if they *want* to, of course."

"We'd love to." Frank Goolz stood up and helped clear the table. "I'll give you a hand with the cooking."

"Nothing too spicy," Suzie said pointedly. "And if there's any broccoli, I'm out of here."

Mum shook her head indignantly. Frank Goolz smiled and winked at Suzie, and they disappeared inside.

I waited for them to be out of earshot, then went back to my phone. "The legend says that the monster is actually the daughter of an English settler," I read.

"What do you mean?" Suzie came closer to look at the screen. "Like she was born this way? Or did a witch curse her?"

"No witches," I told her. "It says she was bitten by some kind of snake, then transformed into the monster and escaped into the marsh."

I found another drawing of the Mallow Marsh Monster. In this one, it was attacking a man in the marsh. The poor guy was screaming, holding an old lantern in one hand and something unexpected in the other. "Why is this guy holding a mirror?" I asked and the Goolz girls came closer to see the picture.

"I don't know," Ilona said. "Maybe he wanted to show the monster just how damn ugly it was before it ate him alive."

"The guy got it all mixed up," Suzie said. "Mirrors are for vampires. For monsters, you need harpoons, fishing nets, and pizzazz."

"Amen," Ilona said, and we went inside for dinner.

4

CRYPTOZOOLOGY
FOR
BEGINNERS

Ilona and I were walking home from school, talking about all kinds of things, like monsters and comic books and how unimaginably boring our English teacher, Mrs. Richer, was. But mostly, we were talking about the foot and how gruesome and puzzling it was.

"If it doesn't belong to Mrs. Farrell, then whose foot is it?" Ilona asked. "And what happened to the bones? That's another pickle."

"And what about the message carved inside that abandoned car? *I'll be back for you.*" It made me shiver each time I repeated it. "Creepy."

We had reached the path alongside the beach. I looked out over the ocean at low tide. The sky was dark gray, and it was hard to make out the line separating the water from the sky.

"I get it," Ilona said. I realized she was looking at the ocean with me.

"What?" I asked.

"I get why my mom loved this place so much. It's beautiful."

"Beautiful," I repeated, though I had stopped gazing at the ocean and was watching her as she drowned her large dark eyes in it.

We walked silently. I ran a mental slideshow of all the extraordinary things that had entered my life recently. It was a surreal mix: A real ghost. A magic stone. A monster plopping body parts in the dark water of the marsh. And Ilona. Mostly Ilona.

"No way!" she shouted, pulling me out of my loopy dream. We had almost reached our houses. She started running toward an ancient, brownish, beaten-down station wagon parked in front of their yard. "That's Uncle Jerry's car!"

"Who's Uncle Jerry?" I called after her.

She twirled around to face me. "He's not really our uncle. We just call him that. He's one of Dad's best friends. He's pretty out there."

"Give me specifics."

She patted the station wagon as affectionately as Han Solo patting the *Millennium Falcon*. It was rusted, banged, scratched, and crusted with mud, and the inside was packed with a mess of plastic bags, old tools, and wadded-up garbage.

"Do you have any idea how many monsters we chased in this car?"

"No."

"Well, plenty." She smiled fondly. "Uncle Jerry is a cryptozoologist. Do you know what that is?"

"Yeah," I said. I had seen plenty of cryptozoology videos on YouTube. "It's like someone who goes around with a night-vision camera, trying to get a good shot of Bigfoot."

"Pretty much. He's a monster hunter." She opened the gate to their yard. "But he likes to see himself as a scientist, even if he doesn't have a degree to prove it."

Suzie came out of their house, bouncing with excitement. "Uncle Jerry's here!" she shouted, hopping down the porch steps. "He's going to stay with us. Dad asked him to come help us find the Marsh Monster." She grabbed my hand excitedly. "Come on, Harold! You're going to love him. He has a weird old flashlight thingy that kills vampires. He says he's going to let me use it on the neighbors' cats and dogs. Oh, I can't wait for tonight!" She let go of my hand and ran back inside.

I took out my phone and called Mum.

"I see you, Harold!" she said playfully, answering my call.

I turned to our house and saw Mum waving at me from the kitchen window.

"I'm going to stay at the Goolz's until dinner. Is that all right?"

She was quiet for a while, mulling it over. "Okay, then. I'll call when dinner's ready."

I hung up and looked back at the window. Mum waved nervously and managed to smile. She was trying to hide how worried she was even after establishing this new truce with our strange neighbors.

"When you meet him, remember not to stare. He hates that," Ilona said as we went up the ramp to their house. "And don't laugh, no matter what he says. Or you're in real trouble. He's very sensitive."

We went through the door and were greeted by a fog of horrible odors—like a mix of BO and moldy clothes, with undertones of rotten foot. Crates and boxes were still lying all over the hall, but the ones in the living room had been pushed against the walls. In the empty space were a cot, a kerosene lamp, and a pile of dirty tools. The room looked like an archaeological site.

Right in the middle of the mess stood a giant man,

sniffing what looked like a slice of salami. "You're right, my friend. There's a distinct funk to it."

Uncle Jerry didn't look like a scientist—not the way I pictured one, anyway. He wasn't frail, bespectacled, and giggling at the wonder of the universe. He looked like an oversized lumberjack on his way to kill grizzly bears with his bare hands. He was huge, with a thick white beard and slicked-back, thinning gray hair. He was as tall as a tower and bulky with muscle. His huge hands and thick fingers were covered with fading tattoos and looked perfectly designed to squash large objects. He wore extra-extra-large khaki cargo shorts and a screaming blue-and-pink Hawaiian shirt.

It was really hard not to stare.

The giant man pinched the slice of salami and stretched it between his fingers. "This is not normal human flesh . . . Oh, hello, darling," he added, noticing Ilona. His gaze lost its warmth as he turned to me. "And who are you?" he asked suspiciously, but didn't bother waiting for an answer.

He picked up a dish containing the human teeth we had collected in the pickup truck and dropped the slice of salami on top of them. It wasn't salami, I realized. It was the slice of severed foot that Frank Goolz kept in their freezer.

Frank Goolz put a hand on my shoulder. "This is Harold!" he said with a flourish. "He's a good kid. And he's one of us."

"All right, then," Uncle Jerry said, looking at me sideways like he wasn't convinced. "But he's your responsibility. If he gets maimed, killed, or eaten, don't blame it on me."

"Harold's awesome," Ilona said. "He saved us when we got locked under a kitchen floor. He's a natural."

My heart went *pop!* and my face started radiating a thousand degrees of blushing heat.

"Do you know how many times I've heard that story? *Hey Jerry, this guy's awesome. Oh, can he join our team?*, and then *POOF!* Someone loses an eye, and everyone starts pointing fingers and yelling at me."

Uncle Jerry took a red paper napkin out of his breast pocket. But instead of wiping his fingers with it, he tore off a large chunk, threw it in his mouth, and started chewing.

"Show him the pictures of the foot, Harold," Frank Goolz said.

I took out my phone and pulled up the photos. Uncle Jerry snatched it away from me. I wished he had wiped his fingers first.

"Ha! Not human! So obvious." He kept swiping

through the pictures, sneering at each one. "You did good calling me, Frank. The Mallow Marsh Monster is awake, and that foot might be the first piece of proof."

"You truly believe the Marsh Monster exists, like for real?" I asked, and the giant gave me a hard look.

"Kid, I'm a biologist and a Marsh Monster expert, all right? I've written tons of books on the subject. I've got a dozen copies in the back of my car, and I will sell you one for a good price. I'll sign it too." He turned to Frank Goolz. "We need the whole foot. Where is it?"

"I gave it to Ed Farrell. He's the father of the twins with the missing mother. He's a doctor. He said that the foot is part of his scientific research."

"Ha!" Uncle Jerry handed me back my phone. "Doctors! What do they know? They have all the diplomas, but not the brains." He tapped his giant head. "That's more my department. I'm a math genius. Did you tell the kid that?"

"Uncle Jerry's brilliant," Ilona confirmed. "He knows everything about UFOs, Atlantis, Cryptocreatures, Hollow Earth, ancient aliens . . ." She ticked them off on her fingers. "And he's saved us so many times."

"You bet." Uncle Jerry sat down on his cot. It squeaked painfully and nearly folded in half under his weight. He scratched his beard, thinking.

"What about those teeth?" I asked.

He picked one up and tapped it on the lip of the dish a couple times, listening carefully to the noise it made against the porcelain. "Fake! Obviously. Just like that phony foot."

"You mean they're not human?" I looked at Frank Goolz for a second opinion.

"Well. First day of school for you, kid." The giant man threw another piece of paper in his gigantic mouth and chewed it thoughtfully. "People don't get that about swamp creatures. They're magical beings—shapeshifters. It probably disguised itself as human to lure this Feral woman—"

"Farrell," I interrupted. "Mrs. Farrell."

"HEY!" he yelled at me, bouncing on the cot and nearly giving me a heart attack. "Frank! Tell the kid not to interrupt me or I'll bite his nose off."

"Uncle Jerry doesn't like it when you ruin one of his stories." Ilona came close to me and put a protective hand on my shoulder. "He's passionate. But don't worry. Your nose is safe when you're with me. Isn't that right, Uncle Jerry?"

"The boy just needs to learn some manners," he told her, his voice softening as he spoke to her. "And I'm not telling stories. Everything I say is factual, dear."

"So?" I asked hesitantly, instinctively pinching my nose. "The foot? The teeth? They belong to the monster?"

He gave me a long, dark look. Clearly, I still had a long way to go before he accepted me as a member of the outfit. "If *you* had let me finish, you would know by now," he snapped. "But yes. Those are not the remains of Mrs. . . . FARRELL." The cot took another serious blow. He took the dish and gave the slice of foot another deep whiff. "They are human imitations that the creature shed when it shape-shifted back into the Marsh Monster. I'll bet you my hat on it."

"Uncle Jerry? Can I play with the vampire Zapo-thingy, now?" Suzie came back from the kitchen with a plate of Ilona's horrible homemade cookies. She was already chewing on one.

"It's not a toy, dear." Uncle Jerry swallowed a mouthful of napkin and grabbed a couple of cookies from the plate. He threw one in his mouth and swallowed it like a pill. He licked his fingers—the very same ones that had touched the rotting flesh just an instant ago. "Giovanni's Vampire Zaporino releases the light of a thousand suns all at once. It would atomize a vampire or any other sun-fearing demon in an instant."

Frank Goolz picked up what looked like an ancient, rusted flashlight.

"Look, Harold. That's the vampire lamp!" Suzie gave the plate of cookies to Ilona and held out her hand. "Can I have it?"

"It's not a lamp and it's very dangerous, Suzie." Frank Goolz looked at the strange symbols carved all over it. "Giovanni was an Italian alchemist. He was obsessed with vampires. He's the one who invented the Zaporino."

"A Zaporino!" I smiled at Ilona. "It's a funny name for something you use to fight vampires."

"With a name like that, quite a few of them must have had a laugh before being blasted out of existence," she agreed.

"It's part-science, part-magic. And Jerry's right. The Zaporino is not a toy." He handed it to Suzie anyway. "Just don't press the trigger. We would all go blind for a very long time."

"Cool." She pointed it at an ancient stuffed owl staring at us from the top of a bookcase. "*Zaaap!*"

"Seriously, Suzie. Do not press the trigger."

Suzie ignored her sister and pretended to zap each corner of the room. "If the monster attacks us, I'll just . . ." She turned to zap an imaginary monster in the hall, then yelped and dropped the gadget.

Suzie stepped backward until she was safe against her dad, who put an arm around her.

"Oh, shoot." Ilona forgot the plate of cookies in her hand. A few slid off and smashed on the floor.

The cot squealed painfully as Uncle Jerry stood up.

The Farrell twins stood silently in the hallway right outside the living room. Who knew how long they'd been standing there, listening to us? They weren't carrying a shoebox this time, but they looked even more afraid than when they'd brought the boneless foot.

"I bet they found another body part," Suzie said.

Their gray dresses were torn, their tights no longer white. Their hair was caked with black slime, like they'd been wrestling in tar.

"It took Dad," they said with a freakish calmness.

"The Marsh Monster."

"It came out of the floor—"

"In Dad's lab—"

"In the basement."

"And took him away."

5

THE
THING FROM OUT
THERE

Ilona and Suzie were upstairs looking for clean clothes to give the twins. Frank Goolz and Uncle Jerry had gone to the Farrells' house to look for Mr. Farrell and maybe have a close encounter with the monster.

I switched on a floor lamp. It was getting dark outside, and I was alone with the twins in the Goolz's living room. I turned to the large window and looked into the twilight. An eerie chill ran through my body as I realized that an impossible creature like the Mallow Marsh Monster could actually be roaming around out there.

"Is she your girlfriend?"

"Like her little sister says?"

"We like her little sister."

"We like your girlfriend, too."

I shrugged uneasily. "She's not really my girlfriend. I don't think." I took a breath to steel myself before asking the only question that mattered to me. "Did you see the monster? Did you see it for real when it took your father?"

"As real as we see you," they said as one.

One twin was sitting on a crate, the other standing by her side. They looked particularly unsettling in their dirty, torn clothes, and with their hair full of black goo.

"What did it look like?" I switched on another lamp, trying to fight away the darkness and fear.

"Its skin was all green."

"And slimy."

"It had claws."

"Huge ones."

"And pointy teeth."

"Lots of them."

"And enormous red eyes."

"And shiny scales."

"All over its body like a snake."

"And feathers—"

"Like this."

They both held their hands up by their necks, fingers outstretched.

"Its screams hurt your ears."

"It screamed and screamed and screamed—"

"When it dragged Dad into the well in his lab."

"It kept screaming—"

"A long time after they were gone."

"Crap," I said. I tried to turn on the third and last light, but the lightbulb was dead.

"Do you think the writer—"

"And his big friend—"

"—will find our parents?"

"Oh, I'm sure they will," I lied. I turned at the sound of Ilona and Suzie clamoring back down the stairs. They came into the living room with armloads of clothes.

Suzie dropped a pile on a crate. "We took a bit of everything. We weren't sure what you'd like."

Ilona added another pile on top of Suzie's. "Go on, dig in."

The Farrell sisters looked at each other with alarm in their eyes.

"It's all right," Ilona insisted. "You can wear whatever you like."

Ruth pinched a pair of jeans and Beth pulled out a pink T-shirt. They looked at the clothes like they were filth.

"We can't wear these."

"Or those."

"Except if you have two of something."

"And they're *exactly* the same."

"Then maybe we'd like it."

"Otherwise . . ."

"*Nuh-uh!*"

They dropped the clothes back in the pile.

"Why? They're just jeans." Ilona eyed the twins' dirty clothes. "There are lots of dresses in there too."

"We always dress exactly the same."

"Always!"

"Can't you make an exception for tonight?" Ilona asked.

"I'd die if I had to dress like Ilo all the time," Suzie said. She picked up one of Ilona's long black dresses. "She's like a mini-Morticia. Don't you think so, Harold?"

I loved how Ilona dressed and was about to say so when a huge *CRACK-BOOM* resonated through the house. It sounded like the house had been hit by a big rig.

Ilona and I looked at each other, and I saw my fear mirrored on her face.

"Cheese!" she said.

"Crap!" I answered.

Suzie screamed and ran to Ilona's side. "I saw it!" she yelled, pointing at a window. "I saw it looking at us!"

My blood froze, and I turned to the window, expecting to see a monster grinning at us.

"We saw it, too!" the twins yelled.

They had retreated to the other side of the room, as far away from the windows as possible. They were holding each other in terror.

Ilona and I looked from one window to the next, but there was nothing but darkness outside. "Are you sure you saw it?" Ilona asked Suzie.

"Yes!" she shouted. "It was BIG and . . . and nasty and . . . and STUPID GREEN!" She pulled Ilona away from the windows.

"Define *big*," I said, rushing to join them.

She spread her hands as far apart as she could. "I mean, *really big*, Harold. And it had these huge eyes, like fly eyes, if the fly was the size of a building. Staring at us like we're its next snack!"

"Oh, great." I kept my focus on the windows. The world out there was gone. No stars. No moon. No more twilight. All I could see was the reflection of the five of us packed together and scared. "Are you sure you saw what you saw?"

"Didn't you hear me scream?" she barked at me, as

69

if a Goolz wouldn't scream for anything less than a bug-eyed monster outside a window.

I suddenly realized that the front door wasn't locked and zoomed toward it. The lock was a little high for me. I reached for it, pushing against the arm of my wheelchair. I could just barely touch it with the tips of my fingers.

"I'll do it," Ilona said, picking up Uncle Jerry's Zaporino thingy from where he'd left it on top of a crate.

"I got it." I gave a final push to lift myself as high as possible. I was nearly there when—*KABOOM*—the door nearly jumped off its frame.

"CRAP!" I yelled.

"Get away from the door!" Ilona ran to it and locked it.

I reversed away from the door at top speed.

"It must be huge," I said.

"Did you see it?" Suzie asked, coming into the hall with the twins.

The twins were shaking so much that large flakes of dried mud were falling off their faces.

"We want our parents—"

"Now!"

That thing out there, it probably has your parents . . .

70

inside its stomach! I thought, but I didn't say it because I didn't want to make everything even worse for them.

"Stay away from the door and the windows," Ilona shouted at us, inspecting the Zaporino to figure out how it worked. "That has to be the trigger, right?" She showed me a brass button on the base. "I guess you just press it and . . . and that's that."

"Do you think it'll kill it?" I asked.

"NO!" the twins shouted.

"We're scared!"

"*I* am scared!" Ruth said, breaking from their usual *we-as-one* speak.

"It won't work." Suzie's face looked drained of blood. "It's not a vampire."

"But . . . Uncle Jerry said this lamp's packing serious blasting power," I reminded her hopefully.

"Uncle Jerry's a great guy, Harold. I love him to bits. But let's be honest." Ilona knocked the end of the Zaporino on her forehead. "Uncle Jerry's bananas."

"Shut up," Suzie whispered. "Did you hear that?"

Ilona aimed the Zaporino at the door. We were all staring at it, waiting for something to happen. Everything was still and silent except for the dull cracking of the wooden boards under our collective weight. And then—*CRACK-BOOM*—the thing from out there

71

rammed against the door again and nearly split it in two. We produced a chorus of yelps and shouts.

"Mommy, mommy, mommy . . ." The twins sobbed, hiding their faces against each other's trembling shoulders.

"Suzie, go upstairs with them. Lock yourselves in Dad's office. And stay away from the windows." Ilona gave her sister a shove. "Now, Suzie! NOW!"

"FINE!" Suzie groused. She grabbed the twins by the arms and the three of them ran upstairs.

We heard a door slam and lock. And then it was eerily silent.

"We'll be fine, Harold," Ilona said. "If that creature tries to get in, I'm zapping it."

"Oh, crapola!" I yelped suddenly.

"What?!" she yelled, losing some of her cool.

My phone had started vibrating inside the pocket of my hoodie. I checked the screen. It was Mum.

"Dinner's ready," she trilled when I answered.

We're the dinner, I thought. I could hear loud classical music in the background and thanked my lucky stars that it must have been drowning out the sounds from the Goolz's house.

"Tell her to lock her door," Ilona whispered. "And ask her to go to her window and check our house."

"I made savory pancakes, you lucky boy. With béchamel. No mushrooms, plenty of cheese, just the way you like it."

"Hold on a second, Mum." I muted my phone. "If she looks at your house and sees a huge green monster, she's going to freak out."

"Ha!" Ilona shook her head and sighed. "Fine. Don't tell her anything. We'll deal with this on our own."

I unmuted.

"Harold? What's going on? Why did you put me on hold?"

"Oh, just . . . stuff!" I tried to sound casual, but my voice was a couple notches too high. "I'll be home soon."

My eyes were locked on the door. I was pretty sure I could hear the creature moving around on the porch. Its paws or hoofs or whatever kind of nightmarish limbs were *clickety-clack*ing against the wooden boards.

"Don't be too long. Pancakes!"

"Yeah!" I cheered weakly, trying to match her enthusiasm. "I'll be there in a minute."

I hung up and the creature stopped moving. It rapped the base of the front door. I saw the tips of two long black claws slide through the tiny gap on the floor. They moved left and right, exploring the gap, and then disappeared. My heart was pounding so hard that my head moved to the beat. My eyes were locked on the large split running vertically down the front door. Could it sustain another blow?

It didn't matter. A window imploded in the living room. The monster had chosen another way in. We heard something heavy land inside and thrash around in broken glass.

Ilona ran to the living room door, slammed it, and leaned against it. "Harold!" she shouted.

The monster crashed against the door, nearly tearing it off the wall on the first blow. Ilona fell to the floor as if she had been hit by a car. The Zaporino flew out of her hand. She grabbed it and crawled to me on all fours, then leaned against my legs and pointed it at the door.

We heard the *clickety-clack* of the creature's claws moving around in the living room. Then silence. Then the doorknob started to turn.

"Don't you just hate it when monsters have opposable thumbs?!" Ilona complained.

The lock clicked. The creature pushed on the door. It had fallen half off the hinges, so it got stuck midway.

"You go back to hell!" Ilona took aim, but didn't press the trigger. Her hands were shaking. She looked frozen with fear.

I snatched the Zaporino from her. Something green and scarier than death was leaning into the hall to take a look at us. I saw its head. I saw its jaws. I saw its paws and its claws. I saw its bulging red grapefruit-sized eyes. It roared when it saw us. I aimed the gadget and squeezed my eyes shut.

"Close your eyes!" I shouted to Ilona.

I pulled the trigger. There was a long hiss and *ZAAAAP!*

The room was flooded with the intense white light of a thousand stars. The creature shrieked so high it hurt my ears. I tried to look at it, to see if the Zaporino had done enough damage, but I couldn't see a thing.

"Harold!" Ilona called. I felt her hand pressing against my chest, making sure I was still there with her. "I can't see!"

"Me neither."

I could hear the creature moving around. My fingers groped for the trigger.

"Shoot it again."

"I'm trying to." And then I screamed as something tried to drag me out of my wheelchair. I felt Ilona grab hold of my hoodie, but I was jerked out of her grip and hit the floor, landing hard on my back. My fingers somehow found the trigger. I covered my eyes with my left arm and pulled the trigger. There was another long hiss and a radiating *ZAAAAP*. The monster screeched even louder. I heard it thrashing madly.

"Harold, where are you?"

I recovered some of my sight and saw Ilona crawling toward me.

"I see you," she said. She leaned over me and touched my face like a blind person trying to figure out my features. "Tell me you're all right."

"I think I am," I said. She helped me to sit up.

My vision was slowly coming back. I looked around for the monster, but didn't see it anywhere. "I think it's gone."

We stayed there, silently listening. The only sounds were the wind and the ocean waves—and then my phone vibrating in my pocket again.

"Harold! Seriously!" Mum complained when I picked up her call. "The pancakes are getting cold and my béchamel is getting dry."

"Sorry," I said breathlessly. "Time flies when you're having fun. I'll be there in a sec, I promise." I hung up.

The twins' voices floated down from upstairs.

"Is it safe?"

"Is it dead?"

"Is it gone?"

We looked up and saw them standing with Suzie at the top of the stairs.

Suzie took a step down. "Tell us!"

Ilona turned to me with a smile. "Harold got the monster."

She looked so impressed, so proud, so madly in love with me that my throat tightened and words didn't come out easily.

"I got it good," I confirmed.

6

THE
BITE

"It wasn't supposed to be so dry." Mum was stirring her béchamel hopelessly. "It was perfect. And then it got overcooked."

I didn't care about the béchamel fiasco. I was sitting with her at the dining room table, looking out at the veranda, thinking about the monster: Claws. Jaws. Gigantic red eyes.

"You're not eating," she complained. "It's not very good, is it?"

"No, it's delicious." I soaked a morsel of pancake in the overcooked béchamel and forced it into my mouth.

It was pitch-dark outside. The windows had turned into perfect black mirrors. The ocean had disappeared, replaced by our own reflections. The monster could be out there, looking at us, and we wouldn't know it.

"Harold?" she said. "You're so quiet. Is everything all right with the Goolz?"

"Everything's fine. They're great."

I remembered how Suzie had knelt and dipped her fingers into the black goo on the living room floor. "Is that the creature's blood?" she'd asked. "Did the Zaporino make it bleed?"

"Harold!" Mum called me back to the present.

"What?"

"You don't have to eat it if you don't like it. I can warm up something else."

I put down my fork and smiled at her. "The pancakes are fine, but I'm really not that hungry. I snacked nonstop at the Goolz," I lied. "Can I leave the table?"

She sighed and nodded.

I carried my plate to the sink and scraped the uneaten pancakes into the trash bin. I tried to see the Goolz's home through the window, but could only see my own face and worried eyes. My mind was racing in circles—from the monster to Ilona's face, and back to the monster.

I squinted at the window. "What the hell?" The reflection of my face had suddenly morphed into Ilona's features. Then I realized it wasn't a reflection—Ilona

79

really was there on the other side of the window, close enough that I could see her despite the glare.

She waved and pointed toward the drainpipe she sometimes used to secretly climb up to my bedroom on the second floor. She disappeared into the dark before Mum saw her.

"I'm going upstairs." I pushed away from the sink and zoomed to the stair lift.

"Snacking is not eating!" Mum called as the lift carried me up. "Is there *anything* the Goolz do right?"

"Scaring people!" I called back.

"Ha!" Mum sneered and shook her head. "They don't scare me."

I reached the landing and shifted my body into my chair, then went to my room and closed the door behind me. Ilona was already perched outside the window. I opened it for her, and she slid gracefully into the room and brushed the dirt from her dress. I looked out. A light came to life on the Goolz's porch. Uncle Jerry came out, carrying a bunch of planks and some tools. He dropped them in front of the broken window and got to work boarding it up.

"They didn't find Mr. Farrell," Ilona said from beside me. "Uncle Jerry was terribly disappointed that he missed the monster attack."

We watched him nailing a board across the lower part of the window. I could see his butt crack despite the distance. I closed the window, but we could still hear the sharp raps of his hammer.

"I hope Mum doesn't ask what happened to your window."

"Didn't she see or hear anything?" Ilona pushed aside some of the mess on my bed and sat down.

I shrugged. "I guess not."

"Good. I like your mom, but we have to keep her in the dark, or she'll never let you out of the house again."

She swung her legs up on the bed and leaned against the wall. "The twins are going to stay with us tonight," she said, adjusting my pillow behind her back. "You know what? I think the monster was going after them. That's why it came all the way from the marsh to our house."

"*I'll be back for you*," I said, quoting the message carved in the truck. "I thought about that too. But how did it know where to find them?"

She shrugged. "Dunno."

"Why is it going after them?"

"Dunno."

I heard Mum's percolator bubbling downstairs. The smell of brewing coffee drifted into my room. Coffee at night meant Mum was going to be working late.

I switched on my bedside lamp so we could see each other better. Ilona looked down at my leg and her eyes went wide. "What is that?"

"What's what?" I looked down. "Oh, crap!" Black goo had soaked through my jeans and was dripping onto my white sneaker. I checked the floor behind me and saw that I had left an inky trail of black spots from the window to my bed. "Is that coming *out of me*?!"

I lifted the leg of my jeans and Ilona got off the bed to squat in front of me.

"Harold!" she exclaimed. "Did that creature *bite* you?"

"I don't know," I said. "I wouldn't have felt it. It dragged me out of my chair."

She pointed at a messy circle of gray punctures. "That looks like a bite!"

I leaned down to look. Instead of blood, the holes oozed black goo.

"It bit me!"

Ilona collected some of the goo with her finger. "This looks like the goop the monster left behind after you zapped it." She sniffed it. "It smells like moldy wood." She looked up at me. "We have to wash out the wound."

"Bathroom!" I barked and made a sharp turn toward the door. I wanted to get rid of that evil slime as fast as possible.

Ilona followed me into the hall. We stopped, listening for Mum. She was humming while doing the dishes. I nodded at Ilona and we proceeded into the bathroom.

Ilona took one of the towels hanging by the sink and wet it with warm water. She sat on the edge of the tub, gently lifted my leg onto her lap, and carefully cleaned the wound. In no time, the white towel looked like it had wrestled with a squid—and lost.

"Is it still coming out of me?"

Ilona threw the towel on the floor. "I don't know."

She took another towel and patted my leg dry, removing the last traces of black sludge.

"Maybe it's nothing," she said when she was done, but her voice sounded shaky. The little gray dots, no bigger than mosquito bites, had stopped oozing.

"Maybe it's nothing," I repeated. We looked at each other. She looked as scared as I felt.

We heard Mum coming upstairs, still humming. Ilona pulled down the leg of my jeans and carefully took my leg off her lap. She sprang up and picked up the filthy towel right as Mum passed the open bathroom door.

"Oh!" Mum cried. "Ilona! How long have you been here? How did you get in?"

"She climbed through my window," I said. Ilona gaped at me, but I was too freaked out to think of a lie.

Mum looked at Ilona, who was holding the two darkened towels behind her back. "I just needed to talk to Harold," Ilona said. "School stuff."

Mum put her coffee cup down on a small table in the hallway and crossed her arms tightly over her chest. She was so busy being annoyed at us and staring down at Ilona that she missed the black spot on my jeans. "This is not okay, you two. Ilona, I'm walking you home right now."

"I can go by myself," Ilona said.

"You're not getting off that easy. I'm going to speak to your father about this."

Ilona nodded. She dropped the towels on my lap as soon as Mum turned her back to us. I discreetly tossed them into my bedroom as I followed them to the stairs.

"I'm coming with you."

Mum stopped on the landing. "No, you're not, young man. You stay here and wait your turn."

"It's okay, Harold. I'll see you tomorrow," Ilona said. I nodded and watched them go downstairs.

Just before going out, Mum looked up at me. "Not

cool!" she said and slammed the door behind them.

I lifted my jeans. The bite was dry. The skin had a reddish glow around it. I touched it. It was radiating warmth. I quickly pulled my jeans over it, as if not seeing it would make it go away.

"Not cool," I repeated and waited for Mum to return and reinstate the embargo.

7

THE
MONSTER WITHIN

I woke up feeling great.

I sat up in bed and pushed away my duvet with a rare energy. I was so full of beans, I felt like giving myself a high five and *woot-woot*ing for joy.

I remembered the monster and the bite and Mum scolding me about Ilona, but none of it seemed to matter. "This is awesome!" I shouted, without even knowing what exactly I was so happy about.

I checked my leg. All traces of the monster bite were gone. I pressed down on the skin—it wasn't even sore. It was like it had never happened.

I shifted my body into my wheelchair and went to the window to check for any unusual activity at the Goolz's house. The sun came in so hard when I opened the curtains that I felt like it had slapped me. I threw the curtains closed. Back in the darkness, it took only a nanosecond for the feeling of unlimited strength to flow back into me.

I picked up the soiled towels from the floor and stuffed them in my backpack, planning to trash them on my way to school. "Sorry, guys. You didn't survive the monster attack," I told them and zipped the bag. I picked up my jeans next. I studied them and decided that the dried black spot wasn't odd enough to alarm Mum. "You, you survived it," I said, and dumped them in the laundry basket on my way to the stairs.

I stopped in the hall to take in the lovely scent of pancakes and bacon coming from downstairs. "Wicked," I said. I was ravenous. Suddenly my goal in life was to stuff my face with food, and pancakes and bacon seemed perfect.

"Did you sleep at all?" I asked Mum as I rode the lift downstairs.

Mum turned around, and I had my answer. She looked exhausted, her eyes empty, her bathrobe defeated, her shoulders slumped like they were pulled by an excess of gravity.

"I did an all-nighter," she said. "My brain is mush."

She set a plate in front of me as I pulled up to the

table. "Accounting is not for the faint-hearted." She yawned. "This is a pancake rerun. I had so much left-over batter."

"Awesome! The award for best mum in the world goes to YOU." I also wanted to high-five her and *woot-woot*ed some more.

She dropped a few pancakes and strips of bacon onto my plate. I looked up at her as she covered them in syrup. Smiling, she looked less tired. She was really pleased with her best mum award.

I grabbed my fork and got to work.

"Hey, easy there, try to chew them at least."

I gave her a thumbs-up as I swallowed a strip of bacon whole. Chewing was for wimps.

"Good to see that last night's shenanigans didn't kill your appetite."

I didn't care that she'd found out Ilona sneaked in or that she'd reported it to Frank Goolz. Knowing him, he'd probably congratulated his daughter for it. As for me, I'd gotten away with nothing but a talking-to. She'd made me promise that from now on, Ilona would use the front door. And that was that.

"I really don't like that strange man living with them." Mum sipped her tea, looking at the Goolz's house through the kitchen window. "He nearly attacked me when I asked him a few simple questions."

She was, of course, talking about Uncle Jerry. He had called her nosy and told her to mind her own business when she'd asked about the window.

"Who falls through a window anyway?" she asked me, since Frank Goolz had told her that his giant guest had tripped on their porch and fallen through the glass.

"He's big and clumsy," I said, using my finger to mop up the last traces of syrup on my plate. "Could you make more pancakes? I'm really starving today."

She gave me a surprised look and went back to the stove to start another batch.

I sat back, waiting for some sort of relief from the food I had devoured. But the hunger wasn't going away. "More bacon, too," I said. "Please," I added when she gave me a look.

I went to the fridge as she poured batter into a sizzling pan. I opened it and stared in awe. "OJ. You're dead!" I told the bottle and grabbed it with an evil monster laugh.

. . .

After eating enough pancakes to slow down a strong pony, I got ready for school. Ilona was waiting out front, schoolbag in hand, when I went out to the porch.

"Suzie's not coming?" I asked as I joined her on the road.

"She's faking sick again. She wants to stay with the twins. She loves weird people." She looked down at my leg. "How's the bite?"

"It's gone. *Poof!* Like it never happened."

"No more black goo?"

"Not a drop. It was nothing."

She stopped and shook her head. "*Nuh-uh*," she said, mimicking the twins.

"What?"

"It didn't look like nothing to me."

"Well, it was." I lifted my black track pants. "See?"

She leaned to take a closer look. "You're right. It looks fine."

My stomach produced a roaring growl. "Sorry," I said. "Too many pancakes."

She laughed, I pushed down the leg of my tracksuit, and we continued on our way to school. I was going fast, too. I was full of high-octane pancake calories and I wanted to escape the sun on the open road.

"Are you in a hurry to get somewhere?" Ilona had to trot to keep up with me.

"Yeah, I decided I love school. Can't wait to get there."

I darted down the boardwalk and slowed as we

reached the town square. A large crowd of Bay Harborians blocked the path ahead.

"Hey, English boy!" Alex Hewitt called, waving from the edge of the crowd.

Alex used to be the most horrible person in all of Maine and probably the world. He was a skinny boy, short in size and mind, and a couple of years older than us. He used to be a bona fide bully and my worst enemy. But since the Goolz and I had saved his life, he had changed his ways, stopped harassing me, and had even maybe-kind-of-almost become a friend. He still called me "English boy," but it didn't sound like an insult anymore.

"What's going on?" I asked him.

"People are nuts, that's what." He spat on the sidewalk and said some choice words about Bay Harbor and Bay Harborians in general. Changing his bully-ways was going to be a long process.

"Elaborate." Ilona went up on her toes to try to see what was going on. "How nuts?"

"Total bonkers cuckoo crazy nuts. They say the Mallow Marsh Monster is real. Like you and me real!"

Ilona and I looked at each other. She shook her head. There was no point telling him that they were totally right about that.

"Some dudes say they saw it last night. And then

Ms. Pincher's dog goes missing. And some other dude says he saw the monster dragging it into the marsh. I never liked Ms. Pincher's dog anyway. It always barks at me when I walk past her house."

Mayor Carter stepped up on the bed of a pickup truck and spoke to the crowd through a megaphone, spelling out a plan to organize groups to search the marsh. "And don't go shooting everything like it's duck season! I'm talking to you, Glen!"

Mayor Carter was a short, stocky, middle-aged woman with tons of confidence and charisma. Her family had founded Bay Harbor two centuries ago. She also ran our public library and was the curator of the Heritage Museum, which housed a collection of fishermen's memorabilia and old knickknacks. The museum was also Mayor Carter's home. She was one of Mum's favorite people in Bay Harbor. She was one of almost everybody's favorite people.

"Madame Mayor! Are you coming with us into the marsh?" someone shouted.

She nodded and smiled uneasily. "Wouldn't let you have all the fun for yourself, Johnson!"

She was dressed in fisher-hunter gear like the rest of them. Except her clothes looked newer and neater, like this was the first time she'd worn them.

"Everybody, be extremely careful," she said through the megaphone. "We could be dealing with a rabid dog. Or a very dangerous boar."

"THERE ARE NO HOGS IN MAINE!" someone shouted. "We know exactly what took that dog into the marsh. And it's not an oinker!"

Mayor Carter put a baseball cap over her short hair and readjusted her horn-rimmed glasses. She looked nervous as she scanned the crowd for the screamer.

Someone near us said, "It's the Mallow Marsh Monster, and we all know it!"

"Damn right it is," someone else grumbled.

"Just be careful," Mayor Carter continued into the megaphone, ignoring all the monster chatter. She switched off the megaphone and came down from the pickup.

"She looked scared," Ilona said.

"Yeah, she did." Alex snuffled disgustingly and spat on the ground. "I haven't seen her upset like that since we put a stink bomb in her mailbox." He laughed, enjoying the memory, and we continued on our way to school.

. . .

"Are you all right?" Ilona whispered later that day in Mrs. Richer's English class.

"What?"

She picked up a pencil and scribbled a note on the bottom of a page in her textbook: *You were moaning. What's wrong with you?*

"I'm fine," I whispered.

I hadn't noticed that I was moaning. I was watching a fly buzzing around the windows. I felt restless and ravenous, and I couldn't wait for class to be over. I was full of energy and as hungry as a bear in spring. Watching the fly had been a way to stop focusing on the *tick-tick-tick* of the clock.

"I'm just bored," I said, forgetting to whisper.

Mrs. Richer shot me a dark look.

I picked up my pencil. *Hungry. Bored. Time has stopped*, I wrote in my own textbook.

My stomach produced a massive roar and I burped as loud as a bomb.

"Sorry," I told Mrs. Richer. She'd had to stop reading when the entire class started laughing.

"Good one, English boy. Respect!" Alex was laughing the loudest.

The bell rang. I took it as a blessing. I grabbed my things and zoomed out of the classroom and down the hall to my locker, not even bothering to wait for Ilona. I opened my padlock with shaking hands.

"What's the rush?" Ilona asked, catching up with me.

"I'm just starving, that's all." I opened my lunchbox. It was tragically empty. I had eaten all the leftover pancakes I'd brought during first break. At lunchtime, I had devoured half my ham sandwich after giving Ilona the other half. We almost always shared my lunch since our school had no cafeteria and Frank Goolz wasn't really the type of father to keep the kitchen stocked with lunch food.

I licked my finger and collected the crumbs at the bottom of the box, then suckled that finger like my life depended on it. Ilona stared at me, horrified. I must have looked crazy, or plain disgusting.

"It's empty," I said awkwardly.

It was more than empty. It was spotless. I forced myself to put it back in the locker.

"Longest day ever," I said. We still had to go to PE before we could go home.

We headed to the sports field to join the rest of our class. It was sunny outside and the light hit me hard. I quickly put my hood up and shielded my face with my hand.

"Why is it so bright today? It's burning my eyes," I said.

"It's just a nice sunny day," Ilona told me. "And now it's official. There's something seriously wrong with you." Her gaze drifted to my leg, where the monster had bit me.

I didn't want anything to be wrong with me. And if something *was* wrong, I didn't want it to have anything to do with that bite.

"I'm perfectly fine," I insisted. "I just need to go splash some water on my face and I'll meet you on the field."

Ilona nodded. "Go splash that water, and *you* become *you* again." We tried to smile at each other, but it didn't take away her concerned look or make me feel any less worried.

I stopped right before reentering the building and turned to watch her walking toward the field. She wasn't even dressed for sports like the rest of the class. She was just wearing her usual black dress, long black coat, and leather boots. It was her standard outfit, whether she was fighting monsters or playing soccer.

. . .

The bathroom smelled like its usual mix of bleach and cheap yellow soap, but it was especially sickening that day.

"Nothing is wrong with you," I told myself in the mirror, but I knew it was a lie. There were so many things

96

that felt different. The mad hunger, the restlessness, and this new intolerance for sunlight. I splashed water on my face, then cupped my hands to bring some to my mouth. The tip of my tongue hit something sharp as I swallowed.

My heart did a free fall in my chest. "Please, no," I whispered. I ran my tongue over my gums, then opened my mouth wide and put a finger inside to confirm what my tongue had discovered.

Little pointy spikes were pushing on the soft skin right behind my teeth. I ran my finger over them again and again. I tried to convince myself I was imagining things, but I knew I wasn't. There was no doubt about it. I was growing a new set of teeth. More like fangs. A tingling sense of doom crawled up my spine.

The worst thing wasn't that there was a monster in the marsh. The worst thing was that I was turning into one.

8

SAVE ME
FROM
ME

I rushed to the sports field, holding my hood closed over my face like a vampire. Ilona was sitting on the bleachers, watching the other kids run.

"Why are you hiding your face?" she asked when I reached her.

I tightened the hood even more. "New fashion statement. You like?"

"It depends. Are you hiding a massive pimple on your nose?"

"No." I didn't want to tell her about my fangs. I was hoping futilely that they would just go away if I ignored them, but I couldn't stop running my tongue over the little spikes.

"Then I like," she said with an exaggerated French

accent. "It's very next season *Invisible Man je ne sais quoi.*"

"Hey, Harold!" our PE teacher, Mr. Bianco, called. "You and the new girl take a lane."

Mr. Bianco was a really nice man. He was never awkward around me and never treated me any different than anyone else—which meant I never got to sit on the sidelines.

He looked up from his stopwatch as Ilona and I crossed the field.

"Do you realize that your clothes aren't appropriate for exercise?" he asked Ilona.

"Says who?" she responded, taking position beside me in a lane.

"Most people in the world."

Some of the girls sniggered. They all wore various styles of oversized hoodies, leggings, and sneakers on a PE day. As for Mr. Bianco, he was always dressed in tracksuits ready for a jog.

"Never been a trend follower." Ilona lifted her dress with both hands to bring the hem over her knees and got ready for a good run in her leather boots.

Alex was in the lane next to ours. He looked at us and shook his head. "I really want to say something snappy about you guys, but I won't."

Before he renounced his bullying ways, he would

spend all of PE waiting until Mr. Bianco wasn't watching so he could kick my chair and verbally attack me. He left me alone now, but every once in a while he seemed to want credit for it. I ignored him.

My hands were shaking as I gripped my wheels. I still had my hood up and a ball of fear was rapidly expanding in my stomach. It had nothing to do with the race. I needed to tell Ilona about the teeth. We needed to leave school and do something about it. And if this was a nightmare, I needed to wake up.

"Okay, go!" Mr. Bianco said, and we went.

I could see Ilona from the corner of my eye and Alex, a little further back. He was pushing hard, determined not to let us weirdos win. The finish line wasn't far—a hundred yards ahead. The students who had already raced were sitting on the ground beside it, pinching off grass and throwing it at each other out of boredom. A few looked over, then more, and then everyone was watching. Several of them stood up. They weren't bored anymore.

I was going faster and faster—push, *push*, PUSH. All the energy that had been building up in my body throughout the day was surging through me. My heart was pumping powerfully. Fear was transforming into rage, rage into steam. My hood flew off my face. I was clenching my teeth, old and new. I couldn't see Ilona anymore, or Alex, or any of the other students in the race.

I zoomed past the finish line and raised my arms in victory. All the students were standing now. I thought they were going to start cheering. They didn't.

I turned around to see how much distance I'd put between myself and the others. They had all stopped halfway and were staring at me. Ilona still had the hem of her dress in her hands, like she'd forgotten she was holding it.

I looked around. All eyes were still on me. Mr. Bianco's mouth was half open. He finally remembered to click off the stopwatch.

"What got into you, English boy?" Alex shouted, breaking the silence. "Rocket fuel?"

Ilona let go of her dress. Mr. Bianco recovered and told me to get a drink. I headed across the field, feeling every pair of eyes following me.

• • •

"What on earth was that, Harold?" Ilona asked as we started for home. "Did you turn into that rocket man from your comic books?"

"He's called the Flash."

She waved off my attempt to school her about

superheroes. "Whatever. The point is that you got bitten by the Marsh Monster and now you're all sorts of strange."

I stopped and finally found the courage to tell her about the new teeth growing inside my mouth.

"Are you sure?"

I nodded. They felt bigger than they had in the bathroom—like they were ready to pop out and start biting.

"And the sunlight. It's getting worse. It's like liquid acid now."

She nodded. Anyone else would have thought I was, in Alex's words, "total bonkers cuckoo crazy nuts," but Ilona had seen plenty of weird stuff, so she believed me.

"Dad will know what to do," she said. She was doing her best to sound cool and composed, but she sped up until she was nearly running.

We stopped by my house first, so I could ask Mum if I could go next door. She made me promise about a hundred different things, including that I wouldn't ruin her dinner for the second night in a row.

Speaking of food . . . I was grabbing everything that was lying around the kitchen and swallowing it as Mum talked. A piece of bread on a plate on the table. The rest of the banana she'd been eating, which she'd set on the counter as we came in. A fistful of Cocoa Puffs that I poured directly into my hand over the sink.

"Harold! There's food at my house too," Ilona said pointedly.

The food at Ilona's was always awful, but I was so hungry that I didn't mind.

"Okay," I said, accidentally spitting some puffs on the counter and refilling my hand for another fistful on the go. I followed her out, waving vaguely at Mum over my shoulder.

• • •

I immediately recognized the putrid smell as we entered the Goolz's home. It was like bad news that kept coming back.

"That was all that was left of him, floating in the marsh," Uncle Jerry said, his gaze locked on the kitchen table.

A pair of black trousers, torn, a short-sleeved white shirt, gashed and soiled with large black spots of monster goop, and a pair of thick-rimmed glasses, one lens smashed, were spread on the table, like an empty shell of Mr. Farrell.

"Dad's going to be lost."

"He can't see."

"Can't read."

"Can't hardly move—"

"Without his glasses," the twins said.

"I took the foot back from his lab," Frank Goolz said. "Jerry needs to study it."

There was a plate on each side of the empty outline of Mr. Farrell. One was full of Ilona's horrible home-made cookies. The foot was lying sideways on the other one. It was even greener and more bloated than when we first saw it.

"Right on." Uncle Jerry had a fork in one hand, and a steak knife in the other. He leaned over the foot and started to cut off a large piece. I was scared he would throw it in his mouth next.

"I hate that foot," Suzie said. She was sitting outside on the top step of the porch, keeping her back to us and the dreaded severed limb.

"We also found this." Frank Goolz picked up a leather-bound book from the counter behind him. "It's Mr. Farrell's notebook. His journal, so to speak."

"He always writes in it."

"When he's done working in the lab."

"He sits."

"He writes."

"And he moans."

"And complains."

They sighed as one.

"Their father knew about the monster." Uncle Jerry pushed the morsel of rotten foot off the plate and started smashing it with the handle of the knife. "We know that for sure now," he said in between blows. "We found a whole lot of sketches and drawings of the creature in his lab. The guy was obsessed with it."

My eyes squinched closed each time he hammered the piece of rotten flesh. I tried to focus on Ilona's cookies. Even if I hadn't known her cookies were always disgusting, the putrid stink paired with Uncle Jerry's enthusiastic foot-pounding should have killed my appetite, but somehow it had no effect on my stomach. I grabbed one and devoured it eagerly, then grabbed a second and a third before I'd even finished swallowing the first.

"I'm telling you," Uncle Jerry hammered and hammered until the green flesh was pulp, "this is not human. This is out of this world." He collected some of the mashed goo on the tips of his fingers and rubbed them together to test the consistency.

Ilona and I stared at him in horror, but Frank Goolz sat casually in a chair with his own foot resting on the table, only inches away from Uncle Jerry and his hammer. "We learned a lot from the journal," he told us, opening it. "Most of the notes are about a large black slug that the Farrells collected in the marsh."

"We found it in their lab, dead, floating in a jar of yellow syrup." Uncle Jerry brought his fingers dangerously close to his mouth, but luckily he only smelled them. "It's bigger than a cat and dark as night. Ugliest slug you'll ever see."

Frank Goolz tapped a page in the journal. "Apparently, Mrs. Farrell was bitten by that specimen while studying it."

"Bitten, huh?" Ilona asked, looking down at me. "Does the journal say it left tiny little holes on her skin? Holes that oozed black goo?"

"Yes," her dad confirmed, looking at her curiously.

"And then magically disappeared?"

"Correct."

"Then, she started to avoid daylight?"

"Did you read this already?" he asked, turning the pages as she spoke and nodding as the journal confirmed each symptom.

"So she got all kinds of weird and really strong and started to eat enormous amounts of food?"

"That's right!" the twins said.

"She was eating and eating."

"And she said she was as hungry—"

"As a wolf!"

I stopped chewing my fifth cookie and forced myself to put what was left of it down on the table.

Frank Goolz went back to the journal. "He wrote that she became incredibly ravenous, and then very sick. He knew her illness was caused by the slug bite. He describes how he was working on an antidote. And then the journal ends abruptly." He slammed it shut. "How do you know all this, Ilona?"

"I know because it's happening to Harold."

Uncle Jerry wiped his fingers on his Hawaiian shirt. He looked at me with something other than suspicion for the first time since I'd met him. "What's happening exactly?"

"Something terribly wrong," Ilona told them.

"You all right, buddy?" Frank Goolz asked me softly.

I tried to answer, but with all the cookie mush in my mouth it came out as gibberish.

"He was bitten by the monster last night," Ilona piped up. "Just like Mrs. Farrell was bitten by that slug. And now, he can't stand the sunlight. He has developed superspeed . . ." She picked up the half-eaten cookie I'd abandoned on the table and held it out as evidence. "He's eating *buckets* of food." She dropped the cookie back on the table. "AND he's growing a new set of teeth!"

107

"More like fangs," I mumbled, then painfully swallowed the rest of the cookie. My throat was tightening. I knew exactly what Ilona was trying to tell them.

"Wait a second!" Suzie bounded into the kitchen. "You mean Harold is turning into a monster?!"

"Interesting." Frank Goolz put Mr. Farrell's journal down on the counter and came to squat in front of me. "Can I take a look?"

I opened my mouth wide and tilted my head back. All three Goolz plus Uncle Jerry and the twins peered into my mouth.

"I can't see a thing," Uncle Jerry said. He fished a tiny penlight out of his shirt pocket. Frank Goolz took it and lit the inside of my mouth.

I ran my finger over my gums to clear away any cookie crumbs. "Yo shee shem?"

I removed my finger and Frank Goolz went in for a second exploration with the penlight. "Yes, Harold. I see them very well."

"Boy, they're wonderful!" Uncle Jerry marveled. He took a napkin from his breast pocket, bit it nearly in half, and sucked it in like spaghetti.

Suzie pushed against her father. "Let me see! Let me see!" She took a good long look. "Woooooowwwwww," she said finally. "He's going full Herman."

I closed my mouth. The show was over. "Who's Herman?" I asked, grabbing another cookie from the plate.

"He's a German guy who transformed into a giant lizard. He escaped into the Berlin sewage system. He's still down there, as far as we know. Right, Dad?"

"Hmm." Frank Goolz gave the penlight back to Uncle Jerry and scratched his unshaven chin.

Ilona glared at Suzie. "He is *not* going full Herman." She put her hand on my shoulder and looked me right in the eye. "You don't have to worry about that, Harold. We won't let it happen."

The twins looked at each other and then back at me.

"Herman?"

"Harold?"

"New teeth?"

"We don't get it," they said.

"It's quite simple." Suzie pointed at the foot. "Your mother was bitten. She went full Herman." She pointed at me. "Then she bit Harold. He's going full Herman."

The twins still looked perplexed so I simplified it for them: "Your mother is the Mallow Marsh Monster. And I'm going to be one too."

"And if she bit your dad yesterday, so will he,

wherever he is." Ilona looked down at Ed Farrell's empty clothes. We all did.

"No."

"It's impossible."

"Mom is not a monster."

"She'd never attack us."

"Or Dad."

"She loves us."

"You're right," I said, suddenly getting it. "She loves you. That's why she keeps coming back for you."

"*I'll be back for you,*" Ilona said. "She's the one who carved that in the pickup truck before she finished her transformation."

"Of course!" Uncle Jerry boomed, chewed-up napkin spraying from his mouth. "It wasn't the monster shape-shifting into a human to lure your mother. It was your mother turning into a monster. That explains that boneless foot." He pushed against it with the tip of the fork. "This is not leftover food from a messy meal. Your mother took it off like a sock when she was transforming and left it behind as she ran into the marsh. She molted like a snake. I talk about that type of metamorphosis in one of my books. I'll sign a copy for you, if you purchase it," he told the twins.

"We don't want a book."

"We want our mother back."

"We don't want her to be a monster."

"Interesting," Frank Goolz repeated distractedly. He was looking toward the front door, which we had left wide open. Through it, I could see Mum sitting on our porch with a cup of tea.

"She's going to be so mad if I turn into a monster," I said.

"Well," he said. "We've upset your mother too many times since we moved in. We have to stop doing that."

"Meaning?" I asked.

"We're not letting you turn into a monster." He turned to the twins. "And we're going to un-monster your mother."

"Hallelujah!" Ilona clapped her hands. "So, what's the plan?"

I threw the cookie into my mouth, chewing eagerly as I waited for Frank Goolz to tell us how he could stop me from going "full Herman" and how to "un-Herman" Mrs. Farrell. There was a long, painful silence. The only things I could hear were my two sets of teeth working on the cookie and Uncle Jerry grinding a napkin between his own single set of molars.

9

I,
MONSTER

I kept my promise and went home as soon as Mum called me for dinner. I ate another truckload of food and went to lie down on the sofa, watching our white ceiling, mulling over monster thoughts and fears, and running my tongue over my new teeth while Mum read a novel in the chair beside me.

Frank Goolz had said they would come up with a plan. I was waiting.

"You look worried again," Mum said. "You always look worried when you come back from the Goolz's."

"Nah. I'm having a whale of a time," I said to kill that conversation.

Dusk seemed to come in an instant, and the ceiling turned all shades of orange and red. I ran my tongue over my gums for the gazillionth time. The tips of the fangs had pierced the soft tissue, and I could taste blood. The palms of my hands itched. The joints of my fingers ached, and each time I moved them they clicked and cracked.

I closed my eyes, though I wasn't tired. I was restless and wanted to try to quiet my body down. I took a deep breath and my stomach produced an enormous, unnatural *RUMBLE*.

Mum dropped her book on her lap. "Well, pardon you!"

I tried to say something, but instead burped louder than thunder.

"Good one, Harold!" came Suzie's voice. We turned and saw her looking at us from the veranda.

There was a knock on the front door and Mum went to open it as I slid back into my chair. The Goolz and Uncle Jerry came into the room with Mum a moment later.

Mum gave Uncle Jerry a dark look. "Welcome to the nosy lady's home, then."

"Oh. Sorry we started on the wrong boot, lady." Uncle Jerry had his next napkin in hand, ready for consumption. "I didn't know who you were. Frank told me you're a stand-up person and one of the last good guys."

"We're spending the night!" Ilona told me excitedly.

"Are you really?" Mum breathed out, taken aback.

"Oh, right. Dad has to ask you first."

Uncle Jerry started eating the napkin. Suzie crossed the living room and plopped down on the sofa, then looked around like she was considering what to steal. She was carrying an elegant white handbag, which she set down beside her. "Can I sleep on the sofa? I would like that."

"*You would like that?*" Mum was getting annoyed fast. "Frank?"

Frank Goolz was wearing his white shirt, black pants, cool leather boots, and long black coat that was almost exactly like Ilona's. And, of course, he carried his leather satchel. It was his usual outfit for a paranormal expedition. Uncle Jerry was in full camouflage.

"Would you mind taking care of the girls?" Frank Goolz asked and explained that he needed to go away for the night.

"Where to?" Mum asked.

"We're going into the Mallow Marsh."

"At night?"

"I need to suck up the strange atmosphere for my next book. It's a writer thing."

Uncle Jerry sneered and rolled his eyes. "Right!

Let's go *suck up that atmosphere*, Dostoyevsky."

Frank Goolz ignored him. "Is that all right with you?" he asked Mum.

"There's no school tomorrow," Ilona reminded everybody. She sat down next to Suzie like it was a done deal. She was carrying a brown paper bag. "Pajamas," she said when she saw Mum looking at it.

"Her pajamas!" Mum laughed warily. She turned to Frank Goolz. He smiled at her. She turned to me. I nodded. She turned to Uncle Jerry. He chewed his paper. She sighed. "Okay, sure," she said. "We'd love to have the girls for the night."

. . .

"Where are the twins?" I asked once Suzie, Ilona, and I were in my bedroom.

"They sneaked out," Suzie and Ilona said as one.

"*Poof!*"

"Departed."

"Vanished."

"*Ha!*"

They rolled their eyes and sat on my bed in perfect synchronicity. I didn't know whether to laugh or shudder.

"They weren't scared of the monster anymore," Suzie said, breaking from their pitch-perfect impression

115

of the twins. "They probably think they can talk it into transforming back into their mother and ask it for a good-night kiss."

"Dad and Uncle Jerry are going to try to get them back before they get bit and turn into two identical mini-monsters."

"Speaking of bitten and soon-to-be monster people . . ." Suzie looked at me sideways. "Is there anything else growing on you that we should know about?"

"No, just the teeth." I clenched my fist and my knuckles cracked loudly. "My hands feel weird though."

"And you burp like an ogre."

"I've been eating a lot."

I went to the window. There was nothing to see outside, no moon, no stars, just endless darkness. I reached for the glass of water on my nightstand.

Ilona got to it first and took it away from me. "About that." She opened my window and emptied the water outside. "You have to stop eating or drinking anything. It will slow down the process."

"The process?"

"Of you turning into a monster." Suzie opened her white handbag. "But if you turn and attack us, we have this."

She fished out a short, ancient-looking stick.

116

"Brilliant. Please tell me that's a magic wand."

It looked like a magic wand, but hollow, like a wooden pipe. It was about half the length of Suzie's forearm and came to a needle-thin point.

"It's Dad's," Ilona told me. "Suzie and I call it the *Sleep-o-Stick*. It's not a wand. It's a blowgun that shoots magical pellets."

Suzie dug deeper into her handbag and took out a little leather pouch and a set of chopsticks, the kind you get with Chinese takeout.

"Why the chopsticks?"

"Fair question, Harold." She untied the pouch and used the chopsticks to pinch out a tiny green marble that glowed softly. "This is the pellet. If it comes in contact with your skin, you're done for."

"You mean . . . done like *dead*? Like it's poison?"

"No, silly. You don't die. You just take a long nap." Suzie dropped the pellet in the opening of the blowgun, then brought the other side to her lips and aimed at me. She puffed her cheeks and pretended to shoot. "*Plop!* You're dead asleep. Hence the name we gave it: *Sleep-o-Stick*."

"We used to play with it all the time," Ilona told me. "But then Dad confiscated it after I accidentally shot Suzie and she got knocked out for a long time."

"It's really fun." Suzie tilted the blowgun over the pouch and the pellet fell back into it. "Dad says it's really old, like medieval something. It was created by a sorcerer. It's black magic. Dad said we could bring it in case you turn into a monster tonight."

She gave it to me and I inspected it. It was made of dark wood and engraved with snakes eating each other's tails. "Does your father have a real plan besides putting me to sleep with black magic?"

"He'll come up with something." Suzie snatched the blowgun back and put it in her handbag. "He always does."

She lay back on the bed, folded her arms, and made a face. "We should be with him right now, looking for the twins and the monster! But this one . . ." She kicked her sister. "She wanted to stay with you, make sure you're all right. Because she's soooooooooo in love with you that it's getting ridiculous!"

"She's just teasing," Ilona said, but her cheeks were turning rose red.

"Everything's different since we moved next door. It used to be Dad, us, monsters and ghosts, and the occasional shape-shifter. And now, it's all feelings and *What would Harold do?*, and *What would Harold say?*, and *What would Harold's mother think?*" She turned to me, sighed heavily, and closed her eyes. "At least if you really turn into a monster tonight, it won't be a total waste of time."

"You done?" Ilona asked her.

"Yes, you guys can go back to cooing." She kept her eyes closed, signaling she was truly done with us indeed.

"Don't mind her," Ilona told me. "She's been a pest since Dad told her she can't go after the twins with him."

"That's cool. I don't mind," I said, though I was blushing, too.

Mum knocked on the door and came in, carrying a tray with hot cocoa. "I made you a treat."

It was proper cocoa, made with milk and topped with mini-marshmallows, unlike the bitter mixture of stale cocoa powder and hot water they served at the Goolz's house.

I took a cup, dying to gulp it down. I looked at Ilona. She shook her head.

I rested the cup on my lap, holding it with both hands, and watched the marshmallows melting into the creamy chocolate.

"Okay, gang. Thirty more minutes and I want to see everybody in bed."

"Sure thing," Ilona said.

Mum left, and Ilona jumped off the bed and took the mug from my hands. She opened the window and the cocoa met the same fate as my glass of water.

Suzie tried hers. "Ugh! Too sweet!"

She sipped it again anyway, and I watched her longingly.

"How long am I supposed to keep this up?" I asked. "I can't starve myself forever!"

Ilona took the cup from her sister's hands and emptied both hers and Suzie's into the night. The local raccoons were going to have a party on the mini-marshmallows. "Dad will be back soon. He'll know what to do." She closed the window and put the empty cups on my desk. "We're all in this together, okay?"

I nodded and closed my eyes, trying not to think about a bunch of raccoons freeloading on mini-marshmallows that were truly meant for me. It wasn't working.

"I'll be right back," I said finally. I went into the bathroom and locked myself in. I swallowed some blood that was trickling from my gums. "We're all in this together," I repeated aloud. I didn't sound as fierce as Ilona. I sounded scared.

Yet, at the same time, the joy I'd felt that morning was still there, looming in the back of my mind. But

I didn't think it exactly belonged to me. It was the monster inside, eager to come out, even as the rest of me was terrified.

I suddenly realized that I was staring at the sink. The faucet. The beautiful drops of water on the cold metal. *No way,* I told the monster. *You're not getting any water, you dork.*

I moved closer. I was just going to splash some water on my face. That was all. I turned on the faucet. The water poured out, twirling and splashing into the white ceramic basin, making a beautiful symphony of tinkling sounds as it disappeared down the drain. The frothing water was glittering with specks of silver.

"Oh, boy," I muttered.

I cupped my hands to collect some. The ice-cold water blessed my skin. I splashed it on my face and, as if by accident, sucked in the droplets running over my lips. I cupped more, brought my hands straight to my mouth, and slurped it down. Then I leaned forward and connected my mouth directly to the faucet, sucking in as much water as I possibly could.

I must have swallowed a gallon before I pushed away from the sink. "Thank you!" I told the running faucet. Then guilt took over and I quickly turned off the faucet. I looked up and caught my own reflection in the mirror. I looked happy, which made no sense since I was deeply disappointed in myself. I was two people at the same time. Harold and the monster. And the monster was smiling.

I looked away.

"This way!" I heard Frank Goolz shout right behind me. Uncle Jerry was screaming a string of curse words.

I spun around and looked for them behind me. There was no one there.

"Frank! It's going to get me!" Uncle Jerry cried.

"Where are you?" I shouted.

I caught my reflection in the mirror again. It was still smiling. "Stop it!" I said out loud and suddenly it did, in the most surreal way. The entire surface of the mirror turned ink-black and my grinning reflection disappeared. I rubbed my eyes and looked at the mirror again, waiting for my vision to clear and show my own face again. Instead, I saw two little shapes moving in the darkness.

I leaned forward and brought my face close to the mirror. One of the shapes sharpened. "Oh, crap!" I shouted. The shape was Uncle Jerry and the other was Frank Goolz.

"Leave me alone, you damn creature!" Uncle Jerry cried.

An inhuman shriek followed and *zoooom!* The bathroom, the mirror, *everything* was gone. I was in the marsh. I was the one shrieking. I was the monster, and I was the one chasing them. I was pushing away high grass, reaching for Uncle Jerry with my claws, ready to tear him apart. And I felt an indescribable joy. Uncle Jerry let loose a high-pitched scream. He turned to me with the Zaporino in his hand. He zapped me and I jolted back to my human body.

I was in the bathroom again, looking at my reflection in the mirror. The shapes were gone, but I knew it hadn't been a dream. The smell of the marsh, the sensation of the freezing water against my body, the pleasure of hunting Frank Goolz and his giant friend were all real memories. "No more water," I muttered and went to the door. I unlocked it, shivering.

"Somebody help us!" one of the twins screamed behind me. "Please!"

"Don't look!" I commanded myself. My heart was punching the inside of my chest.

"HELP!"

I couldn't help it. I turned around and went back to the mirror. It was black again. There were two new shapes behind the glass—the twins, running away from someone or something, screaming as loud as Uncle

Jerry had. "Here we go again," I said, and *zoooom!* The mirror and the bathroom disappeared. But this time, I didn't teleport into the marsh. I—the monster me— was in the Farrells' house, chasing the twins down the stairs at top speed. But I didn't want to hurt them. I didn't even want to scare them. I wanted to take them into the marsh with me. I slid my claws down the hall- way walls, my enormous green body hardly fitting in the narrow space. I sniffed the air, searching for their scent, then spat out black goo. All I could smell was the unbearable stench of the formalin. The twins had disappeared, and I could no longer sense their presence. I howled in frustration.

"Harold?" Ilona whispered, knocking on the door.

Her voice broke the spell. I spun away from the mirror, opened the door, and bolted into the hallway, breathing hard, looking left and right. I was back in my own home, back in my own mind and body.

"Are you all right?" Ilona asked. "I heard you calling for someone."

"I was calling for your dad," I said, closing the door behind me, as if that thin pane of wood could keep me safe. "And Uncle Jerry."

"What!?" Suzie asked from the doorway to my room.

I told them about the visions, the mirror turning

black, the voices, their father running away from the monster in the marsh. I told them it didn't feel like a hallucination. It felt like the real thing.

"There are two of them—two monsters," I said. "I have no idea how I know that, but I do. One is going after your dad and Uncle Jerry, and the other one wants the twins. And . . ."

I trailed off. Ilona was watching me with worried eyes. "I sound crazy, right?"

"Welcome to our world." Suzie shrugged. "Crazy is pretty standard for a Goolz."

"I don't think you're crazy at all," Ilona said.

"What's happening to me?"

"You're becoming one of them. They must communicate that way, sharing one mind. Like a hive thing."

She was right. I had high-def multi-monster vision. "And the twins. They disappeared when I was—when the monster was running after them. Where do you think they went?"

"I don't know. But Dad is in danger and we have to help him."

"Of course we need to help him!" Suzie shouted. "We should never have let him go without us in the first place."

"Wait!" I said as she started toward the stairs.

125

"What?!" she barked back at me.

"Mum is never going to let me go out. I mean she's not even going to let *you guys* go out now that your dad has put you under her care."

The Goolz sisters looked at each other. Ilona nodded like she'd green-lit an idea that Suzie hadn't even said aloud.

"Bingo!" Suzie said, running downstairs.

"What is she going to do?"

"It's okay, Harold. It's really harmless."

"What's harmless?" Then suddenly I knew what Suzie was going to do. She'd taken her handbag with her. "Suzie! Don't you dare!" I shouted, moving at high speed toward the stair lift.

Mum was relaxing on the sofa, a cup of steaming tea in her hand. She looked up from her book. "What's going on up there?"

Suzie had already taken the blowgun and the chopsticks out of her handbag. "Miss Bell, can you put down your cup? I don't want you to burn yourself."

"Don't you dare Sleep-o-Stick Mum!" I yelled, sliding into the lift and starting my slow descent.

"She's just going to go to sleep and wake up all happy and rested." Ilona said from behind me.

"No!"

Mum put her teacup down on the coffee table. Suzie plucked the pellet out of the leather pouch with the chopsticks and dropped it in the opening of the blowgun.

"What on earth are you doing, Suzie?" Mum asked, standing up.

"It doesn't matter what I tell you, Miss Bell. You won't remember anything that happens for about ten minutes before the pellet gets you."

"Pellet? What pellet?"

I was almost downstairs.

Mum looked at me. "Harold?"

"Suzie, don't!" I looked back at Ilona. "Don't let her do it!"

Ilona looked deep into my eyes and then nodded. "Suzie, don't do it," she said. "Harold doesn't want us to."

"What!?" Suzie took the blowgun away from her lips. "What do you mean *don't do it*? Oh, you guys are such killjoys!"

She lowered the blowgun and the pellet fell out. It bounced on the floor, *bling-bling*ing as it rolled all the way to Mum's feet.

"What on earth is that?" Mum crouched down.

"Mum! Don't!"

She pinched it off the floor and looked at it. "Oh," she said softly, letting it go. It *bling-bling*ed and rolled back to Suzie's feet.

Mum sat down. "Your father is going to hear about this." And, *poof*, she gently fell back on the sofa, fast asleep.

Suzie looked back at us. "I didn't do it."

"You Sleep-o-Sticked Mum!" I had reached the bottom of the stairs. I let go of my chair and shifted my body into it.

Suzie shrugged. "I didn't! You saw it. She did it to herself."

"YOU! SLEEP! O! STICKED! MUM!" I approached the sofa, pointing at Suzie and then at Mum with both hands, like a deranged puppet controlled by a hyperactive puppeteer.

Mum's eyes were half closed, her mouth wide open. She was snoring away.

"She's just sleeping, Harold." Ilona gently closed her eyes.

Suzie picked up the pellet from the floor with her chopsticks and dropped it back into the leather pouch. "It was an accident, okay?"

"It was anything but an accident. I can't believe you did this!" I wailed, touching Mum's hand. "Mum?"

"Let me rephrase it for you, Harold." Suzie zoomed toward the front door. "It was a very lucky accident. Because Dad's in danger and he needs us."

Ilona put on her coat. "Harold, she's right. Your mother will be fine. She won't remember anything that happened. We have to go now."

I let go of Mum's hand and joined them in the hall.

"You have to admit it was sort of fun. Your Mom's face when she picked up the pellet!" Suzie made a silly face, opened the front door, and ran out.

"You people are maniacs," I said.

Ilona shrugged. "'To be alive is to be reckless. To be dead is to be safe,'" she said, quoting one of her father's novels. She gave me a bittersweet smile.

"Hey, lovers! Time to fight monsters, remember? You'll have to hold hands later," Suzie called.

I took a last look at Mum. She was sleeping safely on the sofa. I closed the door and followed the Goolz into the night.

10

MIRROR,
MIRROR

We were halfway to the marsh when we saw a beam of light ahead of us. Someone with a flashlight was coming our way. We had to hide—otherwise someone might ask us questions or even take us home and find Mum in a coma.

We got off the road and disappeared into the maze of yards and houses. We found a nice discreet hiding place behind Ms. Collingwood's toolshed and huddled together.

The flashlight was just passing in front of us when my stomach gurgled noisily. *Oh, no,* I thought as a huge balloon of gas pushed painfully against my chest. "I'm sorry," I whispered.

"About what?" Ilona asked and I burped like a nuclear bomb.

Whoever was carrying the flashlight froze.

"Hello?" someone said, and the beam of a light brushed over us. "Who's there?"

I recognized Mayor Carter's voice. She was cursing under her breath. I had never heard her use that type of language before.

"Hello?" she repeated. "Show yourself."

She cursed some more.

My next burp bubbled up inside of me. I clamped both hands over my mouth to contain the eruption.

My chair moved back. All by itself.

I looked over my shoulder. Ilona was pulling me backward. She put her finger over her lips. Suzie was tiptoeing beside her. We were retreating toward Ms. Collingwood's house, inching along the wall as Mayor Carter left the main road, pointing her flashlight at the spot we'd just abandoned.

"I hear you!" Mayor Carter called. "I know you're here."

Ilona kept pulling me back. My wheels were making an awful lot of noise on the gravel path. "We are so busted," Suzie whispered.

I wanted to whisper back that I totally agreed with her, but instead of murmured words, a gigantic burp with all the acoustic characteristics of a demon having a bowel movement exploded out of me.

"Son of a gun!" Mayor Carter yelled and turned her light toward us. We all quickly shielded our eyes.

"Harold?!" Mayor Carter blurted. "What are you doing out here?"

"Can you stop pointing that light at us?!" Suzie snapped.

The light moved away from our faces. As she approached us, I noticed that Mayor Carter was holding what looked like a Ping-Pong paddle.

She put the paddle on the ground and patted my shoulder. "This is not a good night for a stroll, Harold. There's a wild animal roaming through our town."

Mayor Carter was very fond of me. I was a regular at the public library and we often discussed books. She always recommended great ones. Sometimes I told her about authors and books she hadn't heard of, and she would read them and tell me what she thought.

"Does your mother know you're out here?" she asked.

"Yeah?" I lied.

"She totally does, and she's cool with it," Suzie said defiantly. "And if you're out here looking for the monster, well, that's not us, right? So can we go now?"

"A monster?" Mayor Carter gave a nervous laugh. "I'm not looking for a monster. There's no monster!

No monster at all. I'm doing the same thing you are . . . just taking a walk."

I looked down at the paddle and saw my face reflected back at me. She definitely wasn't on her way to a nighttime Ping-Pong game. The paddle was an old handheld mirror with a silvery frame and a faded reflecting surface.

Mayor Carter picked up the mirror. "You kids shouldn't be out here," she said, hiding the reflective surface of the mirror against her jacket.

"We were on our way home," I said, and suddenly tasted blood in my mouth. Lots of blood. I wanted to spit it out, but I swallowed it instead, hoping it wouldn't show on my teeth.

Mayor Carter nodded. "You kids do that." She looked too tense for someone just taking a stroll with an ancient mirror. "Do you want me to walk with you?"

"We're fine. Thank you. We're going to go that way." Ilona pointed at the path beside Ms. Collingwood's house. "Shortcut. Safer."

Mayor Carter nodded and looked at the main road. She looked at it for a long while, then wheezed out a worried sigh and gave me a little tap on the shoulder with her flashlight. "I'll see you at the library, Harold. Bring your new friends."

"Will do." We watched her walk away.

I put a finger inside my mouth and touched my new teeth. They were bigger now. Fully grown. Larger and sharper than my normal ones. "It's getting worse."

"Good thing you didn't turn in front of her. Wrong audience for that." Suzie pressed her hand on my shoulder. "I'll give you another tip, Harold. I learned it the hard way over years of hunting strange creatures. Don't hide and burp!"

"Noted," I said and turned to Ilona. "Did you notice the mirror?"

"I did."

"It's like in the old drawing we saw. Remember?" I kept my eyes on Mayor Carter. The night swallowed her until all I could see was the dancing beam of her flashlight. "The guy running away from the monster held a mirror exactly like hers."

"I remember." Ilona started to walk toward the main road. "She's going toward the marsh. She looks worried. She's up to something."

We followed Mayor Carter's light at a safe distance. We remained silent until she turned off the road and disappeared into the woods.

"Should we follow her?" I asked.

"Let's go to the Farrells' and find Dad first," Ilona

decided. "We'll solve the mirror puzzle with him."

Mayor Carter's flashlight blinked between trees and then disappeared completely, leaving us in absolute darkness. I took out my phone and turned on the light, catching clouds of mini-mosquitoes in the beam.

"It's ironic," Suzie mused, swinging a stick as she resumed walking toward the marsh. "She was probably looking for a monster. She had you right in front of her and she let you go."

"He's not a monster!" Ilona said.

"Yet."

. . .

"I'm sure there are plenty of good sides to being a monster." Suzie counted on her fingers as we made our way through the grass. "One: No more school. Two: No more showers. Three: No one dares to yell at you when you break things." She stopped at three fingers, searching her mind for more perks. "Four . . . No more vegetables. I think we can all agree that the creature looks more like a carnivore. And, um . . . well, five: it's just cool."

"You're not listening to me." Ilona slapped a mosquito on her hand. "He's not going to become a monster. I won't let it happen."

My stomach grumbled disapprovingly.

Suzie rolled her eyes. "Good luck with that." She split the high grass at the end of the path for me. "Are you still starving?"

"I could suck in these mosquitoes like they were candy."

"Please do." Ilona slapped a giant one on her neck. It left a nasty smudge of blood on her skin.

"Do you feel like eating a dog?" Suzie asked, as we passed the pickup truck. "Or something bigger? Like a small person? A kid, maybe? Would you like to kill and devour someone my size? I could point out a few people I really don't like at school."

The rotting pickup looked even more sinister in the crude light of my phone.

"You never go to school, Suzie," Ilona pointed out.

"Exactly! Because there are so many morons there. If Harold ate a few of them, maybe I would go more."

"Can we talk about something else? I'm seriously starving."

Suzie pointed at me. "See? He's starving. Promise me that if you start eating people, you'll only eat morons."

"I don't know, Suzie. Do we really need to talk about this now?"

"Promise her." Ilona squashed another mosquito on her face. "Or we'll never hear the end of it."

I promised her, and Suzie stopped talking for half a second. "How would you kill them?" she asked.

"Suzie!" Ilona and I begged at the same time.

"O-kay! Bor-ing!"

Ilona stopped to look at the marsh. "Can you see where the monsters are? Are you still having visions?"

I shook my head and looked at the house. A weak, yellowish glow came from the windows, like the Farrells preferred candles to electricity.

"Maybe Dad's inside." Suzie trotted to the front door and knocked. "Hello! Anybody here? Dad? Uncle Jerry?"

Ilona went to one of the windows and peered inside. "I can't see anyone." She moved to the next window. "There!"

"What?" I asked.

"The door to the basement is wide open. There's some light down there."

Suzie tried the door. It was unlocked. She opened it and took a step inside. "Dad? Are you in there?"

We followed her inside. I quickly put my arm over my nose. The smell from the mason jars was unbearable.

"Dad!" Suzie called, walking toward the basement.

Two eerie voices answered.

"He's not here."

"It's just us."

"There was a monster."

"But it's gone."

"Holy zowie!" I said. The voices were coming from the jars! "Did you hear that? Are those things talking?"

"I heard them too." Suzie came over to inspect the jars.

"There!" I shouted as something moved inside a large jar.

"What was it, Harold?" Ilona asked.

I pointed my phone flashlight at it. Two pairs of eyes rolled around in two different jars, looking from Ilona to Suzie and back to me. One eye was green, three were brown. "Oh, no! It's the twins' eyes!" I said in horror.

"Yes, and they're still in their sockets." Ilona removed one of the large jars. The eyes weren't floating around in formalin. The twins were hiding inside the wall, looking at us through a large gap in the partition behind the shelves.

"What are you doing in there?" Suzie helped her sister move several more jars from the shelf to the floor.

"The monster was chasing us."

"We hid inside the walls."

"We're good at hiding."

"We hide in the walls."

"*All. The. Time!*"

"It's exactly like in your vision," Ilona told me.

"These girls are cool." Suzie set a particularly large jar on the floor. "I like them."

"The monster looked for us—"

"For a really long time."

"But it couldn't find us in the wall."

"Then it gave up."

"And ran down to the lab."

They both put their hands through the gap and pointed at the basement.

"Can you get out of there?" I asked.

The two hands and all the eyes disappeared behind the partition. We heard rumbling and cracking and shuffling and followed the sounds to the living room. A board shifted at the base of the wall and the twins slid out of the tiniest gap, scraping their arms and legs in the process.

They stood up in front of us. They had collected a few more layers of dirt and spiderwebs on top of their already ruined outfits. They were so caked with dirt, you'd think we were talking to a couple of creepy mannequins in a tacky haunted house.

Suzie took a good look at them and clicked her

tongue. "You two really need a clean-up."

They tried to brush spiderwebs out of each other's hair.

"Have you seen my father and his friend?" Ilona asked. "We think they've been attacked by the monster—or monsters, maybe. There might be two of them."

She looked at me and I nodded. So far, my monster visions had been one hundred percent accurate.

"Did you see two monsters?" I asked them.

"We saw only one."

"It was huge."

"And very scary."

"We tried to talk to it."

"And we called it Mom!"

"But it was too scary."

"Too nasty."

"Ha!"

"So we ran away."

"And it ran after us."

"And when it couldn't find us—"

"It went down there."

We all turned toward the basement. It was dead silent down there.

Suzie took the Sleep-o-Stick and the chopsticks

out of her white handbag. "Hope black magic works on Marsh Monsters." She dropped the glowing green pellet into the blowgun as we carefully approached the basement stairs.

We leaned forward as one body with four worried heads. It reminded me of the time a huge hornet got into the house, and Mum and I, glued side to side, crept from room to room with a rolled-up magazine. We found the curled-up dead bug inside a shoe months later.

"Sounds like it's gone." I brought my chair to the very edge of the first wooden step. All I could hear was the *plink-plonk* of water dripping on metal.

"What's down there?" Ilona asked.

"It's our parents' lab."

"That's where they do all their experiments."

"They cut snakes."

"Mostly."

I couldn't see much from upstairs, but I thought I saw an opening in the floor. "What's that? A trapdoor?"

"Uh-huh!" the twins confirmed.

"Where does it go?"

"Far away."

"Into the marsh."

"Through mud."

"And water."

"Maybe the monster left through there," Suzie said, keeping the blowgun close to her mouth.

Squinting, I identified something else by the trap-door: a metal cage, large enough to imprison a grown man.

"Must be for really big snakes." Suzie went down the stairs carefully, the twins at her heels.

"They never use the cage."

"It's never locked."

"Never closed."

"Always open."

"Always."

"I'm going to need some help," I said.

"I got it." Ilona held on to the handles of my chair and carefully helped me down, stair by stair.

"Awesome. It's like a medieval dungeon." Suzie whistled admiringly.

Ilona brought me over the last step and we stopped there to look around.

"Cheese," Ilona muttered. "What are your parents working on down here anyway?"

"The next Universal Studios classic monster?" I suggested.

The Farrells' lab was Dr. Frankenstein's dream come

true. There were chains hanging from the ceiling and along the damp stone walls. An old dissection table covered with test tubes, scalpels, knives, saws, and dozens of dead snakes in jars stood in the middle of the room. Jumbles of old bottles and gas burners and what looked like an alchemy kit were scattered on a table by the stairs. All the tools looked ancient. At the far end of the basement, chemical formulas and mathematical equations were scrawled on a rickety blackboard.

"I vote for closing the trapdoor." I went to give it a push. It slammed shut with a deafening *BANG!*, making everyone yelp. "Sorry."

I turned to Ilona and saw that she was inspecting a row of sketches of the monster hanging on a wall above an old wooden desk. Some were more accurate than others, but one—the only one in color—was a perfect rendering of the creature that had attacked us.

Ilona touched it with her index finger. "Uncle Jerry was right. That's definitely our monster."

We all joined her. The desk was covered with more drawings: faces, limbs, torsos, hands, claws. Those horrible eyes. Drawing the Mallow Marsh Monster was apparently the Farrells' number one hobby. I picked up one of the head-to-toe sketches. It showed the monster midleap, its arms and claws extended.

"I don't want to be the one to pop your bubble," Suzie nudged one of the twins and nodded at the prodigious pile of monster art, "but your parents are bonkers."

I picked up another drawing. It showed a giant, eyeless slug with a wide-open mouth full of spiky teeth. It looked more like a leech than a snake.

"That's the slug Uncle Jerry talked about," Ilona said. "The one Mr. Farrell wrote about in his journal. The one that bit his wife."

"Uh-huh," the twins said, pointing at a large jar on the dissection table.

"Hell, yeah!" Suzie approached it. "That's so interestingly disgusting."

It contained a creature just like the one on the drawing in my hand—a repulsive, thick, black, eyeless slug at least three feet long, floating motionless in fluorescent yellow liquid.

Uncle Jerry had been right about it too: it was the most disgusting creature I had ever seen.

I dropped the drawing onto the desk like it was poisonous.

Suzie put the Sleep-o-Stick down on the dissection table and examined the mess of medical tools around the slug jar. She picked up a syringe and a medicine bottle. They were both filled with the same yellow liquid that was in the jar. "What's this?"

"I wish Dad were here," Ilona said. "He would have the answers to all our questions."

BONG! We all yelped as someone or something knocked against the trapdoor.

"I think your parents are back for a kiss-kiss good night," Suzie told the twins, putting down the syringe and the medicine bottle and re-arming herself with the Sleep-o-Stick. "I'm warning you!" she screamed at the trapdoor. "It's lights out for anything that comes through that door!"

"Don't Sleep-o-Stick me, darling," someone answered from inside the trapdoor, laughing.

"Dad?!" the Goolz girls said at the same time.

The trapdoor opened, revealing two dark, slimy creatures. One carried a leather satchel. The other carried the Zaporino. It was Frank Goolz and Uncle Jerry, covered head to toe with syrupy black goo. They crawled into the basement and wiped handfuls of it off their faces.

"Oh, everyone's here!" Frank Goolz shook the goo off his hands, leaving large splats on the floor. "What did we miss?"

11

MONSTER TRAP

Uncle Jerry sniffed the jar containing the giant black slug. "Told you. Uglier than Aunt Amy."

He moved to the desk, leaving behind a trail of dried mud flakes.

Frank Goolz was inspecting the syringe and the yellow liquid in the medicine bottle. "This makes a lot of sense. The Farrells spend their lives trying to find that mythical snake. They find it in the form of a giant slug. It bites Mrs. Farrell. She turns. She attacks Mr. Farrell. He turns. Now they're coming back to get their daughters so they can all live together in the marsh." He smiled at us. "It's actually a beautiful story."

"What's in the syringe, Dad?" Ilona asked.

Frank Goolz looked up at the chemical formulas and equations on the blackboard. He squinted like he was trying to decipher them. "Farrell's journal says he was working on an antidote to cure his wife." He showed us the syringe and the medicine bottle. "This might be it."

The twins were sitting on stools at the dissection table, the Sleep-o-Stick and the open leather pouch in front of them. A soft green glow illuminated their faces.

"An antidote is good," I said.

"An antidote is very good!" Ilona agreed.

"Maybe it's an antidote. Maybe it's poison to kill the monster." Uncle Jerry was sifting through the drawings on the desk. "We better figure out which one it is before shooting it into your friend, darling."

"Good point." Frank Goolz put the syringe and the bottle down and returned to the formulas on the blackboard.

"What's this?" Uncle Jerry said suddenly. He picked up something that looked like a small, chalky, black bugle, which had been hidden under a pile of paper. He sniffed it. "I think it's one of those slugs. But dried and turned into a freaking trumpet!" He tried to blow through it.

"Wait, I've seen that before. Lots of times," I said,

moving closer. "It's called the Hand of Chaos—I don't know why."

"You've seen it where, buddy?" Frank Goolz asked.

"The Heritage Museum, at Mayor Carter's house. Mum and I have been there lots of times."

Suzie held up a piece of paper she'd unearthed from the pile on the desk. "Harold's right."

She gave the document to her dad, and we gathered around him. It was a printout of an article about the opening of the Heritage Museum. A photo showed a younger Mayor Carter standing proudly in the middle of the museum. And there, right behind her, the Hand of Chaos was hanging on the wall, where I had seen it thousands of times before.

"What's it doing here?" Ilona asked, looking from the Hand of Chaos in the photo to the real thing in Uncle Jerry's meaty hand.

Frank Goolz took it away from him and turned to the twins. They stopped playing with the Sleep-o-Stick and shook their heads as one, answering his unasked question. They had no idea why an old horn from the Heritage Museum was in their parents' lab.

Ilona took it from her father to examine it, then shrugged and passed it to me. "Any ideas?"

I looked at it closely. It was ancient, black, made of

rotten-smelling dried skin, and shaped like a pretzel. I shook my head. "Not a clue." I put it back on the desk on top of a pile of sketches.

The twins had turned their attention back to the Sleep-o-Stick and pellet. Their index fingers were dangerously deep inside the pouch.

"So if we touch it."

"We go to sleep?"

"We always sleep—"

"Together."

"And wake up—"

"At the same time."

Ilona took the Sleep-o-Stick and pouch away from the twins and handed them to Suzie. "What about Harold?" she asked. "What are we going to do to stop his transformation?"

Frank Goolz looked at me. "I don't know yet. Jerry?"

"Working on it." Uncle Jerry went back to the jar with the floating slug, leaving another trail of gray flakes on the floor behind him. He lifted the lid to take a good look at it.

"Be careful."

"It bites."

"It bit our mom."

"Real bad."

"I'm sure it did. But now it's dead," Uncle Jerry said absently. He dipped his hand in the syrupy liquid and sloshed around, trying to grab the floating slug.

"Nuh-uh!" the twins said and the slug suddenly twitched in the jar. Uncle Jerry jerked his hand out, slammed the lid back on the jar, and backed away from the table, wiping his fingers on his dirty clothes. "I'm fine," he said awkwardly.

"Whatever we're doing . . ." I held out my hand and moved my fingers. The joints cracked and clicked unnaturally. "We have to do it fast."

My body felt too small. My skin was starting to stretch. My monster teeth were taking up more space in my mouth and I felt something pushing against the back of my eyes. I was one click from turning into the thing we were fighting.

"Dad?" Ilona pleaded.

He sat at the desk and picked up the horn, looking at it so closely that I wondered if he expected it to talk.

"If you become a monster," Suzie put her hand on my shoulder, "I'll still consider you my friend. I hope you'll remember that before you start biting."

I turned to Ilona. She was absorbed in her thoughts, her gaze lost on something no one else could see. She landed back in the lab with us and focused her eyes on me. "I've got a plan." She picked up the syringe from the dissection table. "And it's going to work."

We were all looking at the syringe in her hand.

"Now, there's a slight problem with it." She turned to the cage in the corner of the lab. "We need to get real close to one of the monsters. Close enough to inject it with whatever is in this syringe, but without the creature shredding us to pieces."

"Well, that's doable." Frank Goolz followed her gaze and turned to the cage.

"Oh! Of course. Just like how Dad handled the Carcassonne Creature," Suzie said.

"I remember that! It would have dismembered Frank if it wasn't for that shark cage. Happy days!" Uncle Jerry reminisced.

"Oh, boy," I said.

• • •

The trapdoor was the gateway to a deep well that led to a network of muddy caves. Uncle Jerry and Frank Goolz had discovered one of the caves when they were trying to escape the monster. They had crawled through gooey black mud until they found the old rusted ladder and heard the muffled sound of our voices, which guided them to the Farrells' lab.

"The monsters will probably use this as a way to get

in." Ilona tapped the trapdoor with the heel of her boot. "We're going to leave it open for them." She pointed at the cage in the corner of the lab. "I'll be inside the cage with the twins and a few syringes of the antidote, waiting for one or both of the monsters to show up."

"That's exactly how Dad destroyed the Carcassonne Creature," Suzie explained as she filled all the available syringes with the yellow liquid from the medical bottle. "He went into a shark cage and immersed himself in a lake with tons of dead fish around him to attract it. When the creature showed up and attacked him" —she stabbed an imaginary creature with the syringe in her hand—"he injected it. Only, his syringe was filled with a black ancestral poison instead of a yellow antidote."

And we have the twins instead of dead fish, I thought, but decided not to say out loud.

Uncle Jerry bit off a piece of napkin and chewed it nervously. "I should be the one in the cage with the twins this time. After all, I'm the monster expert."

"No way," the twins said.

"You're too fat."

"Big."

"Huge!"

"You'll squash us!"

"Ha!"

"Fat?!" Uncle Jerry pinched an inch of fat on his gigantic stomach. "This is all muscle." He stretched the skin out a bit further. "I just need to lay off the candies."

"We don't have time for you to diet your way into that cage," Ilona said. "You'll be upstairs with Dad, Harold, and Suzie. You'll take half the syringes with you in case the monsters attack from up there."

Suzie finished filling the last one and put the plastic cap over the needle. She carefully set it on a metallic tray next to the seven other syringes she had already prepared.

"I'll keep the rest of them with me in the cage," Ilona explained. "When one of the monsters shows up and tries to get to the twins"—She stabbed her own imaginary creature with the syringe in her hand, just like her sister had done before—"I'll inject it with this. If it's the antidote and if it works, we'll inject Harold next."

"What if this is not an antidote and it's . . ." I looked at the twins and then at Frank Goolz. "It's . . . the same sort of stuff you used on the Carcass-thing."

"Poison!" the twins said.

"That's not poison." Frank Goolz took the syringe from Ilona's hand and turned to the twins. "Your father

153

would never hurt your mother. This is the antidote he was working on, as he wrote in his journal. I believe he wanted to inject the monster with it, but it attacked him and took him away, not giving him a chance to do it." He put the syringe in his coat pocket and took his daughter's hands. "Your plan is brilliant, darling. We need to try the antidote on the monsters, and if it makes them human again, we will use it on Harold and stop his transformation. But once again, *I'll* be the one in the cage when they attack. You'll be upstairs, where you can keep each other safe. That's just the way it's gonna be."

They looked at each other silently while Ilona processed what he'd said. Finally she nodded, and he landed a kiss on top of her head.

"Worst-case scenario . . ." Uncle Jerry dropped four syringes in his breast pocket. "The cure doesn't work and we have two dead monsters and one live one to show the world."

"No one is going to die. Or turn into a monster." Ilona handed the remaining syringes to her father. "It's going to work, right, Dad?"

He smiled at her and unbolted the trapdoor. "You—" He pointed at the twins. "In the cage. Every-one else, go upstairs."

The twins scurried into the cage. Frank Goolz grabbed his satchel and followed them in, then snaked his hand through the bars to turn the key that was hanging from the lock. He removed it and dropped it into his satchel.

Uncle Jerry led the way out of the basement. "You heard the man. Everybody out!"

Ilona grabbed the handles of my chair. "Suzie!"

Suzie ran to the dissection table and grabbed the Zaporino that Uncle Jerry had left there. "Why can't I stay with you down here?" she asked her father. "I'm way older than when we defeated the Carcassonne Creature. Old enough for cage duties."

"Forget about it," Uncle Jerry grunted. "Frank always gets the fun jobs."

"Maybe you'll get lucky," Frank Goolz told her. "The monsters might attack from upstairs." He extended his arm outside the cage and pulled her gently toward him. "Hold on to the Zaporino, my love. It might come in handy. Now go help your sister."

Suzie sighed and put the Zaporino in her handbag with the Sleep-o-Stick. "I have a bad feeling about this," she said, but she did as her father asked and came to help Ilona with my chair. I kept my eyes on Frank Goolz and the twins. The cage was tall enough for the girls to stand up, but he had to squat. He showed me one of the syringes. "We've got this, Harold. You be good up there."

I did a mock military salute as we ascended the last step out of the basement.

"Two monsters! Ha! I haven't been this excited since my beard caught on fire," Uncle Jerry said, bolting the basement door behind us.

. . .

Ilona switched off all the lights except one in the kitchen, so we had just enough light to move around without knocking into things. It didn't make any difference for me. I was silently and secretly exercising my new monster supersenses. I could sense the locations of people behind me and even in the basement. I could even feel their emotions—fear, excitement, impatience.

Suzie was drumming the Zaporino against her leg. The noise it made was unbearable. Closing my eyes only made it worse. I could hear Ilona breathing. I could hear her heartbeat as clearly as if I had my ear against her chest. I could hear Uncle Jerry grinding his teeth and feel the strong current of cool air streaming into his big hairy nostrils, then blasting out in a hot rush.

Even worse was the plink-plonk of the dripping faucet in the kitchen. Each drop was a nuclear explosion, reminding me that I needed to drink or die.

But that wasn't the worst. The worst things were the creepy voices inside my mind. They were like frantic ideas that kept bouncing around my head but weren't mine. *Give us back our daughters, give us back our daughters,* they repeated incessantly. And each time I closed my eyes, I knew for sure that the ideas came from the monsters themselves and that somehow, since I was becoming one of them, they had a way of broadcasting their thoughts directly into my head, just like they had broadcast their own visions earlier that night.

"You all right?" Ilona asked, noticing that I was closing my eyes.

"A-okay," I lied.

Suzie finally stopped fiddling with the Zaporino. "Maybe the monsters are busy eating a dog some-where?" She was sitting on the floor, her back against the wall, staring at the basement door.

"They'll come. I'm sure of that." Uncle Jerry was posted at the window, a syringe in his hand, scanning the darkness outside for any sign of monster activity.

"How long can we wait before it's too late?" Suzie asked. Waiting wasn't her strong suit. She was the type to live in the moment, especially if she could run around breaking things.

Ilona dragged a chair over and sat beside me. She shivered from the cold. Even without looking at her, I could count the goose bumps on the back of her neck, which was both surreal and awesome.

"It's going to work," she said. She nervously shifted her grip on the syringe she was holding. I heard the liquid sloshing back and forth.

"I'm out!" Uncle Jerry shouted, making us jump. He threw the last tiny corner of a napkin in his mouth. "Has anybody seen any paper towels? No toilet paper. I don't chew on that." He stopped on his way to the kitchen and turned to the basement door. Something inhuman had just shrieked down there.

GIVE US BACK OUR DAUGHTERS! a terrifying voice screamed inside my head.

"It's coming through the trapdoor, like Ilona said it would." On top of receiving its thoughts, I could sense its presence and see the creature crawling out of the well.

Suzie jumped to her feet, and I approached the basement door. I put my hand on it. "It's staying away from the cage. I think it knows it's a trap."

"How do you know?" Suzie was holding the Zaporino with both hands, pointing it at the door.

"I just do. I can see it in my mind. I can even hear its thoughts. The monster knows exactly what your father is trying to do."

There was a terrifying cry, followed by a terrible *KABOOM*. I knew the monster had picked up the dissection table and thrown it against the cage with tremendous force.

"We've got to help them!" Suzie shouted.

"Frank!" Uncle Jerry reached for the lock. "I'm coming, buddy."

"No!" Frank yelled from the basement. "Do not open that door."

And the monster shrieked horribly.

"Guys," I said, backing away from the door. I flipped around on my back wheels to look at the dark corridor upstairs.

GIVE US BACK OUR DAUGHTERS! GIVE US BACK OUR DAUGHTERS! two different voices kept screaming in my head.

"There's another one on the roof," I said.

Ilona took up position beside me, syringe in hand, ready to inoculate whatever came our way. "Where is it, Harold?"

"It's trying to find a way in." A window exploded upstairs.

"It found it." Uncle Jerry gulped down the last morsel of paper in his mouth and coughed when it got stuck in his throat. He took the plastic cap off his syringe, and a moment later Ilona did the same.

The alien voices in my head suddenly stopped. It seemed that the creatures could choose when to broadcast their sinister thoughts and when to go silent. Still, I could sense their physical presence and feel how the one upstairs was slowly crawling toward us in the darkness.

"It's going to attack," I said.

"Harold, I am not one hundred percent sure that my plan was such a great idea," Ilona whispered helplessly. The goose bumps on her neck had doubled, and it wasn't from the cold.

"I got this." Uncle Jerry was pointing the syringe toward the stairs, his hand shaking like crazy. "Where is it now, Harold?"

"It's upstairs, looking down at us."

"Should I zap it?" Suzie aimed the Zaporino. Her hand was steady.

The twins screamed downstairs.

GIVE US BACK OUR DAUGHTERS!

The monster leapt down the stairs, aiming for Suzie.

"Suzie! Zap it!" I shouted. "Zap it NOW!"

Zaaaap! The room glowed a pure white light, and pain exploded behind my eyes. I screamed. The monster screamed. The twins kept screaming. It was a real symphony of terror.

"Ilona, it's burning me!" I covered my face. It felt like the skin was being torn from my body. "I'm burning!"

I felt something oozing off my eyes and sliding between my fingers.

Ilona dropped her syringe on the floor and her hands found me. "Suzie, don't use the Zaporino again! It's hurting Harold!"

"It blinded me!" Uncle Jerry shouted. "I can't see a thing. Can anyone see?"

The burning pain was radiating in waves from my face and hands.

"Where's the monster?" Suzie asked.

"Come here to me, child," Uncle Jerry told her.

"Okay," Suzie said.

A moment of silence followed, then Suzie screamed. "Uncle Jerry! It's got me! Ilona! Harold!"

A window exploded in the hall. Uncle Jerry shouted a stream of curse words. Suzie called Ilona's name again and again. Her cries started fading away.

And then, everything went still. Uncle Jerry switched on a light.

"Suzie!" Ilona called desperately. "Suzie! Where are you?"

Suzie didn't say anything. Suzie was gone.

12

CHASING SUZIE

"It knew it was a trap." Frank Goolz threw on his coat. He and the twins had come running upstairs as soon as they'd heard Ilona shouting for her sister.

"It destroyed the lab."

"Broke everything."

"When our dad sees that . . ."

"Our real dad."

"Not our monster-dad."

"He's going to be . . ."

"*Fu-ri-ous!*" the twins said.

I finished wiping the black goo oozing from my eyes with a towel. "I can feel what they feel. I can hear what they think. Maybe they can do the same with me." I threw the towel on the floor. "Maybe they plugged

into my mind and that's how they knew it was a trap."
I turned to Ilona. "It's like you said. Like a hive mind."

"Can you see where they are? Do you see Suzie?
Do you hear what they're thinking right now?" she
asked.

"I can't see where they are." I looked into her eyes.
They were full of rage, fear, and even some tears. I was
about to make things worse. "But I know what they
want."

I could sense the creatures chattering inside my
head about it, the words like noise but their meaning
strangely clear to me.

"They want us to deliver their daughters in the
marsh, and they'll give us back Suzie. Unharmed,
uneaten, and safe."

We all turned to the twins.

"No!" they said as one.

"You can't give us . . ."

"To them!"

"They will bite us."

"Eat us."

"Make us . . ."

"MONSTERS!"

"Of course, we're not doing that." Frank Goolz
retrieved the cage key from his coat pocket and gave

164

it to Uncle Jerry. "You squeeze yourself into that cage and lock yourself in with the twins. Try not to squash them."

The twins didn't dare protest about his size this time.

Uncle Jerry looked down at the key in his hand. "But, Frank! I want to go hunt that thing with you."

"Someone needs to stay in the house with the twins and protect them." Frank Goolz checked his four syringes. "And if the monsters come back, do your best to inject them."

Uncle Jerry started to protest, but Frank Goolz wasn't going to waste any time on pointless arguments. "Ilo! You come with me." He gave Ilona two of his syringes. "You too, Harold! And you stay plugged into their mind and help us find Suzie," he said and ran outside.

Ilona and I rushed out after him.

I looked back at the house as we reached the dock. Uncle Jerry was standing at the door, grumbling and fuming. The twins stood behind him in the hall, surrounded by mason jars filled with dead things, looking disheveled and strange. They waved at me. "Crap," I muttered when I realized they were using opposite hands. Somehow seeing them lose their synchronicity unnerved me more than when they moved as one.

"Harold, hurry!" Ilona called. She was running after her father, their leather boots already pounding a frenetic beat on the wood of the dock.

The dock was connected to the muddy ground like a ramp. I got on it easily and charged full-steam ahead until I caught up with them. They had stopped and now stood side by side, scanning the marsh.

"Can you hear them in your head? Can you see them?" Ilona asked.

The moonlight, obscured by heavy clouds, provided very little light. I closed my eyes, trying to see if my monster superpowers could help us find Suzie.

Water, grass, insects, frogs, the dock, Frank Goolz, the syringe in his hand, Ilona catching her breath . . . They all appeared in my mind with such clarity that I didn't need to use my eyes anymore.

"Snake," I said as one slid gracefully into the water maybe fifty yards away.

"What?" Ilona asked.

"Wait." I sensed something else. Someone was nearby, frightened and alone. "Someone's over there." I pointed into the thick darkness eating up the dock ahead of us.

"Is it Suzie?"

"I don't know. I don't think so."

Frank Goolz gave me a tap on the back and darted forward. We followed him.

"There!" I shouted. Moonlight hit the dock through a break in the clouds, revealing an unmoving shape ahead of us. It was Mayor Carter, balled up in pain and fear.

She rolled onto her back and winced, the old mirror clenched in her hand. "I couldn't make it look in the mirror."

"Did it bite you?" Frank Goolz hunkered down to check her body for bites.

"I couldn't make it look at itself!" she repeated.

"Was the monster dragging a girl? My daughter Suzie? Did you see her?"

She opened her mouth but no words came out. But her bewildered eyes said plenty.

"I don't think she was bitten or hurt. I think she's in shock." Frank Goolz stood up, scanning the marsh again. "Harold, you've got to find her."

"Harold?" Mayor Carter moaned, seeing me for the first time. "You have to make the monster look at itself." She held the mirror out to me.

"I think Mayor Carter lost her marbles," I whispered to the Goolz.

"Never mind about that," Ilona said briskly, scanning

167

the marsh with her father. "Can you hear their thoughts, now? Can you see through the monsters' eyes? You gotta help us, Harold."

I closed my eyes, took a deep breath, and tried to plug into the monsters' minds.

It was silent. No thoughts. No vision. No monsters.

"I . . ."

I opened my eyes when I heard Suzie scream. I didn't need my superpowers for that. Everyone had heard it, even Mayor Carter, who lifted her head to try to see who was screaming with such terror.

Ilona leaned over the railing on the side of the dock and called Suzie's name. The clouds moved in front of the moon, plunging us back into darkness. I took out my phone and turned on the flashlight.

"This way." I balanced the phone against my stomach and moved forward, lighting the way for them.

"Wait! Don't leave me!" Mayor Carter wailed.

"We'll be back for you," Frank Goolz shouted. "After we get my daughter back!"

I was pushing hard on my wheels, my chair throbbing on the uneven boards at a mad tempo.

"Oh, no." I slowed to a stop. The dock ahead of me had collapsed into the water.

Ilona and her father stopped, too, the three of us right at the edge.

"Can you tell where she is?" Ilona asked.

GIVE US BACK OUR DAUGHTERS, the monsters' voices said inside my head. I could also sense Suzie's presence ahead.

"She's there," I said, pointing at the submerged boards.

Ilona called for Suzie again. All we heard back was the echo of her own voice fading over the buzzing of the marsh. "Are you sure she's there?"

"I'm sure." I brought myself dangerously close to the water. Suzie's presence was like a knowing rooted deep inside of me. "She's right ahead."

"What about the monsters? Are they with her?" Ilona asked.

"I don't know. I can't feel their presence right now. But they keep telling me that they want their daughters back."

"Come on, Ilo! We'll find out if they're with her soon enough." Frank Goolz stepped off the edge. He looked back at me. "You stay here, Harold, we'll be back with her," and he sloshed away, hip-deep in the dark water.

"I have to go with him," Ilona said.

169

"I know."

She took the syringes from her coat pocket and handed one to me. "Be careful. If one of them comes near you, inject it."

She jumped into the water. "Hell, it's cold," she breathed out, then followed her father, holding the syringe out of the water.

She looked back at me before disappearing from view, her eyes reflecting the light from my phone. I could hear her heartbeat for a long time after I could no longer see her. Then the sound faded away, leaving only the sense of her presence in my mind.

I put on my brakes angrily. I felt rotten. The image of Ilona disappearing from my sight played on a loop behind my eyes. I made a promise to myself then and there that I would never again let her walk into danger without me.

"Dammit!" I yelled.

I looked down at the syringe gripped in my fist. It was shining in the weak light from my phone. I tapped the flashlight off and put the phone back into my sweatshirt pocket.

A board cracked behind me. A piece of wood broke off and splashed into the water. Something had approached while I was distracted over Ilona. "Mayor

Carter?" I asked, sensing the new presence. I released my brakes and turned around, dropping the syringe in my lap.

"Oh freaking no!" Something was crawling toward me on the dock. A dark cloud moved in the sky and a ray of silvery moonlight brushed the creature's slimy green skin.

GIVE US BACK OUR DAUGHTERS!

And then the Mallow Marsh Monster stood up right in front of me.

13

THE
MALLOW MARSH
MONSTER

Moving away from the creature, even half an inch, meant falling backward into the water.

Five short yards in front of me, things looked even bleaker.

The monster spread its long, thin green arms, blocking all possible escape routes. It took a couple of steps toward me, tightening the distance between sheer terror and absolute doom.

I tried to shout for help, but my throat closed on the words. The monster tilted its head back, opened its enormous jaws, and let loose an ear-piercing shriek, which trailed off in a concert of gurgles.

"Ilona," I managed to croak.

The monster focused its bubbly red insect eyes on

me. Mr. Farrell's drawings were impressively accurate. The creature had a mane of purple and green feathers, which opened and spread around its head.

It approached me slowly, now making a guttural *tick-tack-tock-tock* sound from deep in its throat. I started shivering. My hand groped for the syringe on my lap.

The monster leaned over me. It was so close, I could see its scales moving in waves all over its body. I was repeating Ilona's name under my breath like a prayer as the creature sniffed me through two huge holes in the middle of its face. Warm black goo splattered on my face as it exhaled. I tried to remove the cap from the syringe, but my hands were shaking too much. The monster took my face in its enormous hands and started to squeeze, *tick-tack-tock-tock*ing louder and louder. It cranked my head left and right, like a demented doctor trying to unscrew it.

MONSTER! it concluded inside my own mind when it took its hands away.

Apparently pleased with its diagnosis, the creature jerked its head back, and roared, spraying me with another lungful of sticky slime. My fingers found the plastic cap on the syringe. I flicked it away and swung my arm as hard as I could.

For a moment, the Mallow Marsh Monster and I

stared straight into each other's eyes. Then it looked down at my hand, which was gripping the syringe, which was sunk to the hilt just above its hip.

"Uh . . . sorry," I said. I wasn't an expert in monster facial expressions, but by the way it opened its mouth and showed me its fangs, I knew it wasn't too happy about the syringe situation.

I punched the piston. The monster grabbed the syringe and threw it into the marsh, but I was pretty sure most of the contents had already gone into its body. The creature turned its face back toward mine, suddenly deathly silent.

MURDER!!! the monster screamed inside my head.

"Ilona and her father will be here any second," I told it. "Frank Goolz is nuts and Ilona has more guts than an army of you."

The monster didn't seem to care. It raised both its hands, claws out, ready to shred me to pieces. Its hands went down. But instead of taking my face off, they went to its side where the syringe had been. The monster looked up at me and vomited a bellyful of black slush onto my lap. Its body started to convulse. It fell to its knees and crawled away from me, like I'd become the true monster of the marsh. It looked up, its feathers beginning to wilt, and heaved out another load of slush before running away, ape-like, on all fours.

"Ilona!" I shouted once I could breathe again.

No one answered. I took out my phone and used the light to follow the monster, needing to see whether Mr. Farrell's concoction had worked.

I slowed down when I saw a dark lump ahead of me. It was Mayor Carter, passed out on the dock, her mirror by her side, reflecting the moon.

"Hold on, Mayor Carter. I'll send help," I said, and continued my pursuit.

I reached the end of the dock and struggled through the mud to reach the Farrells' house.

"Uncle Jerry?" I called as I entered. "Ruth? Beth? Where are you guys?"

There was no answer.

"I injected the monster!" I added proudly. "Can anyone hear me?"

I reached the basement door and looked down the stairs. The lab was totaled, black goo splattered everywhere. The trapdoor was wide open and the cage was empty.

"ANYBODY?!" I yelled.

Someone moaned in the kitchen. "Who is that?" I said, lowering my voice.

I peeked through the doorway. It wasn't Uncle Jerry

or one of the twins. It was a half-monster, half-human creature trying to crawl under the kitchen table. I moved closer to get a better look. Patches of green were flaking off one hand, revealing human skin underneath. It used its human hand to pound the side of its head, dislodging one bulgy red eye and revealing a beautiful human eye, looking at me in fear. The half-monster inserted its human fingers under the scaly skin on its forehead and pulled off its scalp, freeing long black hair. The second insect eye fell off all by itself and rolled right to my chair. It turned from red to gray, then liquefied, and finally evaporated in a cloud of acrid smoke. The monster was gone, the only evidence a few gray puddles on the linoleum around Mrs. Farrell's human form.

"It worked!" I said.

Mrs. Farrell curled into the fetal position, breathing calmly—sleeping, it seemed.

"I need to find Uncle Jerry," I said, even though she couldn't hear me.

"Uncle Jerry!" I called, rocketing down the hall. I went back outside, scanning the soggy yard as I continued to yell his name.

"Harold!"

"Over here!"

"Behind you."

"In the truck."

The twins were in the cab of the pickup truck, knocking on the windshield to get my attention. Uncle Jerry opened the rusty passenger door and unfolded his bulky body from the seat.

"The monster attacked us," he said. "And I saved the twins."

"We couldn't get in the cage with him."

"He was too big."

"Like we said."

"So when the monster attacked . . ."

"He punched it—"

"Real hard—"

"Twice!"

"And the monster got all dizzy."

"So we ran out—"

"Fast!"

"And we hid—"

"Here!"

Uncle Jerry puffed out his chest. "Not the first time I had to one-two a monster, kids. I practically knocked out that one!"

I looked down at my hands. They were still shaking from my encounter with the creature. They were also losing patches of skin, revealing green scales underneath.

"Where is the antidote?" I asked. "I need it. Now!"

I pinched my palm, tearing off a large patch of human skin. "I've gotta stop doing that."

"Yes, stop doing that, Harold!" Ilona said from behind me.

I turned around, dropping the patch of skin on the ground. Ilona was stepping off the dock, followed by her father, but no Suzie.

"The antidote works." I nodded toward the house. "I injected one of the monsters and it turned back into Mrs. Farrell."

I looked at the twins. "Your mother's in the kitchen. She's fine."

"Mom!" they screamed and ran inside to see her.

Uncle Jerry followed them. He stopped at the doorway, and pointed a finger at me. "Frank was right about you. You're a good kid."

I was still scratching my monster hand, discreetly removing more skin. Ilona took out a syringe.

"You're sure this works?" she asked.

"Positive."

She removed the cap, pulled the neck of my hoodie aside. "This might hurt."

I closed my eyes and she injected the antidote into my shoulder. A wave of fatigue washed over me.

"How do you feel?" she asked.

"Drowsy," I said. I felt my eyes drifting closed.

"He's passing out." I opened my eyes to see Frank Goolz hunched over me. He lifted me out of my chair. I looked down at my green monster hand dangling against his coat as he carried me into the house.

Frank Goolz put me down on the sofa. He turned to Uncle Jerry and told him to take my wheelchair and go collect Mayor Carter on the dock before she rolled into the water.

The twins' faces appeared right above me.

"You saved our mother."

"She's sleeping."

"Naked."

"But she's fine."

"Thanks to you."

Ilona's face appeared beside theirs. They looked like three fairies bent over a cradle.

"You're going to be fine too, Harold," she said.

"You know what?" I mumbled, my words falling one by one into a bottomless pit. "I beat the monster," and, *poof*, I passed out.

14

A PACT
IN THE
WIND

I woke up and checked my hand. It was normal—pink, familiar, and entirely human.

I looked around. My eyes landed on my Hulk poster, and I realized I was lying on my own bed in my own room. The curtains were drawn, but I could see from the light around the edges that it was a sunny day. Ilona was sitting cross-legged on my desk.

"You've been sleeping forever," she said, giving me a tired smile.

"How did I get here?"

"Dad carried you."

She came to sit on my bed and looked at me closely. "It's over. You're cured."

I instinctively ran the tip of my tongue where my fangs used to be. "No more spiky teeth."

"You spat them out. I tried to keep them to show you, but they dissolved."

"No more monsters' voices in my head, just . . . my own thoughts," I said, looking at her and noticing the fear in her eyes.

"Suzie!" Suddenly I remembered everything that had happened and shot up in bed. "Where's Suzie? Did you find her?"

She shook her head. "Dad and Uncle Jerry are waiting for me downstairs. We're going back to the marsh to look for her. They searched for her all night, but I stayed here to make sure you were okay."

"What about Mum?"

"She's still sleeping like a log."

Ilona went into the hallway to get my wheelchair. I shifted myself into it and we went downstairs.

Mum was curled under a blanket on the sofa. I put my hand on her arm and she stirred, then opened her eyes. "Oh, no!" she cried, sitting up. Her hair looked like an explosion had gone off. Her eyes went from me to Ilona to the veranda and back. "I fell asleep!"

I nodded.

"I slept in my clothes!" She tried to stand, then wobbled and sat back down. She was still Sleep-o-Sticked.

Frank Goolz came in through the open front door. "Ilona, we've got to go now."

Uncle Jerry was standing behind him on the porch. They both looked exhausted and were still covered in dried mud.

"Frank!" Mum said in surprise. "You look awful." She shook her head like she was struggling to stay conscious. "Oh boy, do I need coffee."

Mum's second attempt at standing was more successful. She zigzagged to the coffeemaker. "Where's Suzie?" she asked, struggling to open the tin of coffee.

"Around . . ." Ilona said, putting on her coat. "Thank you for letting us stay over."

Mum managed to pop the lid of the tin and ground coffee spilled on the counter. "Clumsy!" She sighed and turned to Ilona. "I don't even remember falling asleep."

"It's all right, Miss Bell. Sometimes, you just need to sleep."

I followed them to the porch. Uncle Jerry was already getting into his weirdo-mobile. He looked as concerned as Frank Goolz. Ilona lingered beside me. "We have to search every inch of the marsh, Harold."

We knew it was a job she couldn't do with me, but neither of us said anything.

Uncle Jerry's car shuddered and coughed into life, spitting out a nasty cloud of fumes. Frank Goolz opened the passenger door. "Ilona!"

I had never seen him look so worried. He was normally confident and even excited in the midst of horror. Not anymore.

"I've gotta go," Ilona said. "Suzie needs me, Harold."

"I know," I said, but I didn't want her to go. I didn't want us to be apart. My mind was working on over-drive, trying to think of a way to stay together.

We looked at each other silently for a long moment. There were so many things I wanted to tell her. I thought she wanted to tell me a bunch of things too, but she had no time. She had a father and his crazy friend waiting for her and a sister to save from a monster.

She started to walk backward toward the car.

"Ilona."

She stopped, giving me a few extra seconds.

And then, it came over me in a blast of clarity, like a sunrise chasing away the night. "We can do this."

"What?"

"Suzie. We can find her together."

"Harold." She suddenly looked sad.

"I made a promise," I said, struggling with each word. My throat tightened, but I kept talking anyway. "I made a promise to myself last night, and I will keep it." I looked her straight in the eyes. "There's nowhere you will go that I won't go with you."

She looked back at the car. Her father called her again and Uncle Jerry rolled down his window and knocked hard on the outside of the door.

"I have to go, Harold."

"Mayor Carter!" I shouted in a flash of inspiration. I had begged the universe for the perfect solution and it had just popped into my mind.

Ilona tilted her head. "The mayor?"

"Yes, Mayor Carter."

"What about her?"

"The horn from her museum. That old mirror she was carrying. It's the same mirror we saw in those old drawings. She knows something. Something that might help us find Suzie."

Frank Goolz and Uncle Jerry called her again. It was a windy day. Her hair was dancing furiously around her face. It blew into her eyes, but she kept them wide open.

"Okay," she said.

"Okay?"

"Yeah. Okay, Harold," she repeated and walked to the car.

I shivered in the cold while she spoke to them. Uncle Jerry gave her one of the syringes. She stepped back and the car sped away.

She walked back to me once Uncle Jerry's mad-mobile had disappeared in the distance and the wind had carried away its stinking cloud of gray smoke. "We stay together," she said and my heart exploded in my chest. "We can go to Mayor Carter and see if she knows something we don't."

I was blinking, ready to blame the wind if a tear ran down my face.

"Breakfast?" Mum called from the porch. Her mad hair got madder in the wind and she shivered.

I cleared my throat and quickly wiped my eyes. "We already had breakfast," I lied. "We're going to the Heritage Museum."

"Lovely place," Mum said. "Since you're going there, why don't you get Ilona a library card?"

"Yeah, why don't I?" I went back in the house to grab my jacket, then Ilona and I headed toward the path by the beach.

The twins came out of the Goolz's house as we passed. They waved and Ilona waved back. She told me that they had spent the night at their place with their recovering mother. "Dad said that the monster will come after them again tonight, and every night, until the whole Farrell family becomes a bunch of monsters."

"So, we end this today," I said.

"Together."

Forever, I thought, but left it unsaid, focusing on the road ahead.

. . .

At first, Mayor Carter's wife didn't want to let us in. "She's exhausted, guys. She doesn't want to see anybody today."

We begged until she relented and invited us inside.

Mayor Carter was sitting in the dining room, looking at the ocean through a large window. Their house was furnished with antiques and smelled of coffee.

"I wasn't all that brave last night, was I?" Mayor Carter said. She had a blanket over her lap and her hands were shaking. She was turned away from us, and the little of her face I could see was pale.

"You were very brave going all by yourself into the marsh," Ilona said. "Armed with only a mirror to fight the Mallow Marsh Monster."

She finally turned toward us. "Your father and his friend told me that it took your sister. Did they find her?"

Ilona shook her head. "They're at the marsh looking for her right now." She looked at me. "We're searching for Suzie too. We're just following a different lead."

Mayor Carter brought her cup to her mouth as if the

effort pained her. Whatever had happened last night had changed her.

"They won't find the monster in the marsh," she said. "It hides somewhere else. Ed Farrell knew that. That's how it all started."

"Mayor Carter," I said, "if you know where the creature's hiding, you need to tell us."

"Even if I did, you wouldn't believe me."

"We would," Ilona said. "We would believe anything you say, because we know it's all real. The Mallow Marsh Monster is real, and we need to find it to save my sister."

She set her cup on the table. "You're right. The monster is real. And it's my fault that it's back, terrorizing our town after all these years." She stood up. The blanket fell to the floor. She looked like her legs could hardly hold her up.

"The story I'm going to tell you," she said, her hands flat on the dining room table as she leaned toward us, "will make you think I've lost my mind."

15

DOOM
ISLAND

We were rushing toward the marsh on the road to Newton. Mayor Carter had given us most of the clues we needed to find the monster and Suzie.

She had given us her old mirror too. It was stuffed in the kangaroo pocket of my hoodie, the handle hanging out.

Mayor Carter was absolutely right about one thing: No one would believe her story.

Except us, of course.

"Do you think it's still in there?" Ilona asked as we reached the path leading to the Farrells' house.

"Let's hope so."

Ilona parted the curtain of high grass for me and we reached the wrecked pickup truck in record time. It wasn't so spooky anymore. It almost felt familiar.

I struggled through the muddy terrain. Ilona ran ahead to the house, and by the time I made it to the front door, she was already coming back out.

"I got it," she said, brandishing the black horn.

"We've got to find your dad and Uncle Jerry now."

"If we can't, we'll have to find Suzie on our own." Ilona started walking toward the dock and I followed her without hesitation.

I was thinking about what Mayor Carter had told us. She had confirmed that the horn known as the Hand of Chaos used to be in the Heritage Museum—until the Farrells showed up.

"My grandfather gave it to my father, who gave it to me. He told me to never use it, or let anyone else use it," she had told us. "He said it would open a gateway into another world. Another dimension, where the Mallow Marsh Monster used to live. He said that his ancestors had destroyed the creature and all of its kind long ago. He told me never to open the gate and never to go into that magical realm; it was infested with horrible dark snakes, crawling everywhere. If one of those snakes bit anyone, the Mallow Marsh Monster would be back."

"Why didn't you just destroy the horn if you knew it could bring back the monster?" I had asked Mayor Carter.

"I didn't believe any of it, Harold. My ancestors did. They believed that the Mallow Marsh Monster lived in between two worlds—ours and a magical one in the marsh. They believed that the monster traveled between dimensions, stealing men, women, and children from our town. They used the horn to punch a hole in our reality, to hunt the monster on the other side. The horn was a symbol of power for them. They would proudly display it to the villagers, reminding everybody that they should be feared because they could bring back the monster. For me, it was just folklore and super-stition. A harmless old artifact that most everybody had forgotten. Then here comes this couple. The Farrells. They say they're scientists and offer me a huge amount of money for an odd little horn collecting dust in my museum. So I did exactly what my father told me not to do. I sold it to them. And not a month later, the Mallow Marsh Monster was back."

• • •

I looked at the horn in Ilona's hand as we started down the dock.

The Farrells had come to Bay Harbor specifically to get their hands on the horn and explore the magical dimension, Ilona and I had concluded. They knew the legend and had seen the picture of the horn in the newspaper article, so they knew where to get it. They went into the other realm and brought back a slug that bit Mrs. Farrell and transformed her into the monster that terrorized us.

My wheels went over a loose board. I grabbed the handle of the mirror to keep it from falling into the water just in time.

"The mirror's magic, Harold," Mayor Carter had told me when she gave it to me. "If you point it at the monster, it will send it back to its world with no possibility of coming back into our realm. That's how my ancestor used to get rid of it. That's the only way to get rid of it."

"Mayor Carter will never forgive herself for betraying her ancestors," I said as we reached the point where the dock collapsed into the water.

"If anything happens to Suzie, I won't forgive her either," Ilona said, and called for her dad.

Birds flew off from a nearby shrub. Insects buzzed around us. Creatures of various sizes scuttled on the ground and splashed in the water. Frank Goolz and Uncle Jerry were nowhere to be found.

Ilona and I looked at each other. Then we looked down at the horn clenched in her fist.

"Do it," I said.

She took a deep breath and brought the horn to her lips. I expected it to honk, but it produced only a low hum, almost imperceptible.

"Did you hear anything?" she asked.

"Like, almost nothing. Maybe try again?"

Ilona gave it all she had. Her face turned red, but the sound didn't get any louder. Then I noticed the air at the mouth of the horn. It looked wavy, like it came out piping hot. I looked out at the marsh.

"Ilona, stop!"

"What?" She wiped her mouth.

"Look!"

She looked. "Holy flop! It works!"

The dock was no longer submerged in the water. It extended across the marsh, the boards straight and clean, no longer covered in moss. Ahead of us, a hill protruded from the water, like an island in the middle of the marsh.

"Was that there before?" I asked.

"I'd remember something like that!"

The dock led straight to the hill. Ilona took a syringe from her coat pocket and we crossed into the magical world.

"Do you think your father will be able to find us, if we get lost or can't get out?"

192

She shrugged. "I think we're on our own, Harold."

"What if there are a whole bunch of monsters in there?"

"Then we're in deep doo-doo." She held out her hands—one holding the trumpet, the other the single syringe. "We're not exactly equipped for a massive marsh-monster attack."

The dock stopped at the foot of the hill, the ground around it covered with a thick layer of dead leaves. Giant, petrified tree trunks lay where they had fallen eons ago.

"This place is dead."

"Please, Harold. Don't make it sound even spookier than it is," she said, then shouted her sister's name.

"Should you really advertise our presence like that?"

"I want to find her and get out of here as fast as we can."

"I want the same thing, but let's not wake anything that we'd rather stay asleep, that's all I'm saying."

She put the horn under her arm, the syringe back in her pocket, and moved behind my chair to help me up the hill. I pushed hard on my wheels to make it easier for her.

"Next time, let's battle something that lives on flatter ground," I joked, but she just puffed along.

"Wait," I said. "Look at those leaves." They were moving in waves. Something was crawling toward us underneath them.

We stopped and I put on my brakes. A layer of leaves slid downhill, revealing flashes of black.

"Ugh," I said. "It's more of those giant slugs."

I looked around us. The hill was alive with them. Dead leaves were shifting everywhere, revealing shining spots of slimy slug skin.

"Cheese, no," Ilona breathed out. "They're coming for us."

"Crap!" I took out Mayor Carter's mirror and tried to point it in every direction at once. "This isn't doing a thing!"

"She said it will send the monster back into his realm." Ilona picked up a piece of dead wood and threw it at the moving waves of brown leaves to very little effect. "We're already in its realm, Harold."

"Well, a little less magic," I stuffed the mirror back into my pocket, "and a little more action!" I released my brakes, grabbed my wheels, and we kept going. The only way out was up.

"This is so disgusting." Ilona kicked a pile of leaves and a fat slug flew away. "They're trying to bite me!" She kicked another in the opposite direction. "It's like

Mayor Carter said. They're everywhere."

Suddenly she gasped and shouted, "Harold!"

A slug lifted its head out of the leaves right in front of us, its mouth wide open and full of tiny pointed teeth covered in black goo. "Hell, no!"

I gripped my wheels and pushed as hard as I could. The slug hissed when my chair rolled over its head. Ilona jumped over it and found the strength to run, fiercely kicking leaves left and right, sometimes hitting nothing, sometimes kicking away the thick body of a furious slug.

"This is the most horrible place I have ever been in my life." I turned my chair slightly to roll over a slug that was aiming for Ilona's ankle. "I'm *so* giving it zero stars on Yelp."

The hill was easing into a glade, devoid of leaves. The top of the hill flattened to a surface of bare, dry ground, baked by sunlight.

I pivoted when we reached the center of the clearing.

"They're not following us anymore," Ilona said.

She was right. Some of the slugs were trying to venture out of the leaves onto the plateau, but retreated immediately when the sunlight hit their slimy bodies.

"It's the sun," she said, watching them slug away

from the daylight. "They can't stand it—just like the monsters."

"This isn't the best place for a campout," I said, panning around. Everything was dead: all the trees stood petrified. Nothing alive grew on the bleached ground. No birds were chirping. No insects were buzzing.

Ilona drew in a deep breath and shouted "SUZIE!" as loud as she could.

"Here!" a tree answered.

Ilona ran to it. "Suzie!! Are you in there?" She knocked on the dead bark.

"Yes, and it's disgusting!" Suzie knocked back. "Get me out!"

The tree had no branches. It was a hollow tube of desiccated wood.

"The monster sealed me in with mud."

I touched a darker spot and felt moist soil.

"It made the mud by mixing dirt with spit! It was so creepy! I want to go home! NOW!"

I looked over both shoulders, shaking with fear. "Where is it?"

"Harold, I'm stuck in a tree!" she snapped. "How would I know? Just get me out before the sun goes down!"

I started scratching at the mud with my fingers, but

it was as solid as cement. Ilona picked up a rock.

"Did it bite you?" I asked.

Suzie growled in annoyance. "Are you going to ask me a thousand questions?"

"Just answer him, Suzie!" Ilona struck the tree with the rock, and a few pieces flaked off.

"No, it didn't. What about Harold? Is he a monster?"

"No," I said. "The antidote worked."

Ilona gave me her rock and picked up another one. We started hammering the dried mud, breaking off larger and larger patches. Finally, we punched a hole and Suzie stuck her fingers through it. I caught a glimpse of one blue eye.

"Nice to see you," I said, managing a smile. "We missed you."

We dropped the stones and pulled at the edges of the hole with our hands. Suzie did the same thing from inside. Soon the opening was big enough for her head, and then her shoulders. Ilona grabbed her hands and pulled. They both fell onto the ground.

Suzie sat up, dusting herself off. She was covered in mud and monster tar, her hair glued with dirt into uneven patches, but she smiled. Her mood had greatly improved now that she was free.

"Thanks, guys," she said. She stood and gave me a

big, long hug. "You're the bestest friend in the world." She let go of me and turned to her sister. They grinned. They laughed. They cried. And then Ilona got her own hug.

"I love you, you little brat," I heard Ilona whisper as she held her sister tight.

Suzie let her go and wiped her tears, smearing the dirt on her cheeks. "Did you know this place is crawling with those horrible slugs, like the one in the Farrells' lab?"

"Correct." I pointed at the edge of the glade. "And they're waiting for us."

"I could hear them all night, trying to get me. There must have been like a thousand of them. It sounded like they were knocking their heads against the tree, trying to get in."

Ilona wiped away her own tears. "The monster must be resting in another tree, just like the one he used for you." She took the syringe out. "This is our chance to put an end to this."

I scanned the glade. There were plenty of trees still standing. "We have to find one sealed with mud."

Ilona picked up the rocks we had used and handed one to me.

Suzie picked up her own. "Let's hope the monster

isn't sleeping on a bed of slugs."

I shuddered. "Let's hope not," I agreed, and we each chose a tree.

16

NO WAY OUT

The slugs were restless, forming larger and larger packs in greater numbers at the edge of the glade—a living, wriggling wall all around us.

"Blech, they creep me out," Suzie said, knocking her rock against a tree. "Even if we find Mr. Monster, how are we going to get out of here?"

"One problem at a time," Ilona told her, moving to the next tree.

We had divided the glade into three zones. Each of us was exploring one, looking for a suspicious tree.

"Anything?" Ilona called.

I inspected a new tree. It was clean. "Not yet." I smacked it with the rock anyway.

"Monster, monster, we'll find you wherever you

are!" Suzie slapped a tree in frustration. "Nothing here either."

I stopped and looked at the Goolz girls. We were such a good team, even when everything was bleak and hopeless.

"Guys!" Ilona called, taking a step away from the tree she'd been whacking.

We regrouped with her. The sun-bleached tree was slashed with a darker slit, similar to the one we had smashed to free Suzie.

"That must be it," I said.

"This is the one. Guaranteed." Suzie pressed her finger against the mud. "Let's get rid of that ugly, red-eyed monster for good."

Ilona dropped her rock. "The monster is also Ed Farrell. This is a rescue mission, not search and destroy. We're going to free him from that curse." She took out the syringe and removed the plastic cap. "You two break the mud, and I'll inject the monster as soon as I can reach it."

"Amen," I agreed.

The slugs started hissing disapprovingly. We turned to look at them. They were twisting and turning frantically at the edge between shadow and light.

"They're not happy." I shifted my grip on the stone.

I took a deep breath and looked at Suzie. She nodded.

"Here goes." I lifted the stone, closed my eyes, and smashed it against the tree. A large chip flew away and Suzie struck the second blow, breaking off another serious chunk. We worked on it in turns. She hit; I hit—back and forth in perfect synchronicity.

"You're almost there." Ilona's eyes were locked on the growing gap, ready to stab whatever came out.

I struck the tree one last time and a massive cake of mud fell inside. We stopped. The hole was about as big as an apple and darker than night. Nothing moved inside. All we could hear was the maddening hiss of the slugs going crazy.

"I wish you guys had brought the Zaporino. We could zap it and knock it out." Suzie leaned against the tree, trying to get a look at whatever was hiding inside.

"Be careful," I told her.

She glanced at me. "Relax, Harold," she said. And then she screamed.

A green hand darted out and grabbed Suzie's dirty sweater with its pointed claws. It slammed her against the tree, trying to pull her inside. "Harold!" she cried.

I grabbed the back of her sweater and pulled the other way until the monster's arm was halfway out of the tree. It shrieked in pain and let go of Suzie as the sunlight hit its skin. Suzie crashed into me, my chair tilted, and we fell to the ground, knocking Ilona down with us.

The mirror fell out of my pocket. It landed on the dry ground with a sharp *CLING*. "Crap!" I said.

"Is that Mayor Carter's mirror?" Suzie asked.

I picked up the broken mirror and looked at my reflection. The glass held in place, but it was split in two, displaying my face twice, both of them looking horribly scared.

"Do you think this is really the right time to check for pimples?" Suzie yelled at me.

I wanted to explain to her that the mirror was actually a potent anti-monster weapon, but something screeched inside the tree, calling us to attention.

We looked up at the hole. The monster had retracted its arm inside.

Ilona held up the syringe. It was empty. "I got it."

The monster started thrashing and screaming inside the tree. Suzie sat up and brushed monster goo from her sweater where the monster had grabbed her.

We stayed on the ground, watching the tree as the monster kicked and screamed. White and gray clouds of toxic fumes puffed out of the hole. And then the monster fell silent.

The slugs didn't like that. Some of them got so agitated that they braved the sun. They slid into the glade, oozing black goo, then dried up and died just a few feet from the shadows where thousands of their cousins were waiting for us.

The girls helped me back into my chair. I put the broken mirror back in my pocket, swapping it for my phone. We used the phone's flashlight to look inside the tree. The half monster, half man inside was curled into a fetal position, breathing deeply, just like Mrs. Farrell had after her transformation.

I turned off the light and looked up at the sky. The sun was starting to sink. It wasn't going to protect us for much longer.

"We took care of the monster." I nodded toward the slugs still writhing in the shadows. "Now we have to deal with that situation."

Some of the slugs used the shadows of fallen trees to venture closer. Suzie threw rocks at them. There were so many that she couldn't miss. They jumped and hissed at the impact, then slid a little closer as the sky continued to dim.

"We have to use the horn," I told Ilona. She had slid it up her arm and was carrying it around her shoulder. She nodded and took it down.

"I'll do it," I said. She handed it to me, then stopped me with a hand on my arm just as I was about to blow into the horn.

"Wait."

"What?"

"Mr. Farrell. We need to get him out of the tree and make sure he makes it back with us."

I turned toward the tree where he was slowly turning from monster to human. Then, I checked the sun. It was moving along the tips of the trees, edging down dangerously.

"Let's do it fast then."

Suzie found another rock, and the three of us went to work together on the tree. *Smash, smash, smash* in perfect rhythm. I glanced over my shoulder. The slugs were everywhere, slipping from shadow to shadow, sliding over and around each other, hissing angrily, their mouths snapping open and closed.

"We have to use the horn right now," I said. "And pray it gets us out of here."

Ilona pulled out a large chunk of mud. "We're almost there, Harold."

Suzie swept an armload of dirt from the other side of the opening to the ground. Finally, the hole was big enough to extract an adult body.

"I'll try to pull him out." Ilona took off her coat and stuck her head and shoulders into the gap. "As soon as he's out, you blow the horn," she said, her voice muffled by the hollow tree.

I tightened my grip on the horn and prayed that my escape plan worked.

"I got him!" Ilona yelled. "Suzie, help me!"

Suzie grabbed her sister's waist and pulled. My breath came in quick gasps as I watched the slugs drawing nearer. They were so close now that I could smell their meaty stench.

"Pull me out!" Ilona cried.

"Are you all right in there?" I asked.

"It stinks! And he's heavier than a sleeping tiger!"

She came backward out of the gap, two hands gripped in hers. One was perfectly human, the other still monstrous, and both belonged to Ed Farrell. "Come on, Suzie! Pull!!!"

They pulled hard. Ed Farrell's shoulders and head came out of the tree. His face was still covered with large patches of green scales, but he had lost his insect eyes. The rest of Mr. Farrell's body slid out and dropped onto the dead, dry ground.

"Gross! He's naked!" Suzie yelped, letting go of Ilona.

"Help me, Suzie, let's bring him closer to Harold." Ilona grabbed his monster hand; Suzie grabbed his human hand; and they dragged him over to me.

"Harold, blow the horn," Suzie said.

The glade was almost entirely dark. Safe from the sun, the slugs were coming faster. Suzie stomped on the head of the first one to reach us. "Do it, Harold!"

I brought the horn to my mouth and gave it all I had.

"Are you doing it right?" Suzie kicked another slug. "I can't hear a thing."

"Everybody hold hands," Ilona said. She was still holding Mr. Farrell's monster hand in her right and she grabbed my wrist with her left. Suzie lifted Mr. Farrell's hand, which she'd let drop heavily onto his body, and reached out for my other wrist. We were a perfect circle of desperate beings, trying to escape an ocean of slugs by playing an antique horn. Our lives were weird.

I took a deep breath and blew with all my might.

"Do you hear that?" Ilona asked.

"I still don't hear anything!" Suzie answered.

"I don't mean the horn. I mean the water."

I lowered the horn and listened. "I hear it. It sounds like waves."

The slugs stopped moving too. They looked transfixed, like they were listening, too.

"It's a river," Suzie said. "Where did a river come from?"

"Look!" Ilona pointed to the edge of the glade. Water was rushing in from all sides, climbing up the hill and beginning to flood the flat ground around us.

I looked down and saw that my wheels were already half sunk in dark water.

"We're sinking!" Suzie tightened her grip on me.

More water rushed in, and we screamed as the glade seemed to zoom down like a free-falling elevator.

Ilona squatted to keep Ed Farrell's head above the water. The slugs were moving in circles, carried by the current. They struggled toward us, but began to fade out of existence. The dead trees disappeared, replaced by high grass. The cursed island was rapidly morphing back into the Mallow Marsh.

"Help me, he's going to drown!" Ilona yelled. Suzie helped her support Mr. Farrell's upper body.

"I'm in trouble here, too!" I yelled as the water kept rising dangerously fast.

But the current stopped and the freezing water stilled. I was submerged chest-high, but drowning was off the list.

I looked around. Insects were buzzing. Birds were chirping. The broken dock was right behind us.

"We're back," I said. We had defeated the monster and rescued Suzie. We were the A-team.

"Oh, banana bun! Something made the trip back with us." Ilona pointed at something moving in the water. It was the slimy body of a gigantic slug, swimming gracefully toward us. It must have been touching one of us when I played the horn.

"Enough with them!" I cried.

"Go back to where you came from!" Suzie added, splashing it with the flat of her hand.

It lifted its head high above the surface and opened its horrible mouth.

I reached for the mirror in my pocket. It was still there and I took it out, brandishing it above water. I held it by my shoulder like a baseball bat, preparing to smack the slug as far away as possible.

The slug leapt into the air, coming straight at us. I screamed—we all screamed—and I swung the mirror at the slug.

POOF!

It vanished midflight, leaving behind an eye-stinging, acrid cloud of smoke. I looked at the mirror. A bright white light shone from the glass.

"It worked!" I told the Goolz girls.

"You kids all right?" someone yelled. "We heard you scream."

I swiveled my head. Frank Goolz was standing on the broken dock behind us, catching his breath. He must have run at top speed when he heard us.

"We're fine! We've got Suzie!" Ilona was still struggling to keep Ed Farrell afloat. "But we've been busy. We could use some help here."

Frank Goolz jumped into the water.

Uncle Jerry arrived next, part running, part staggering, part dying from the effort. He bent over, hands on his thighs, gasping for breath. "Chasing . . . monsters . . . is . . . exhausting!" he said between huffs and puffs.

Suzie let go of me, sloshed over to her dad, and jumped into his arms. He held her tight with one arm and used the other to help Ilona with Mr. Farrell.

"Kids," he said to us. "Once more, you're the real heroes of that story."

"We're the coolest," Ilona agreed, winking at me and making me the happiest boy in all of Maine.

"Darn straight!" Suzie said, resting her head on her dad's shoulder.

"There's no more Mallow Marsh Monster," I said.

"It didn't know who it was messing with." I looked at Ilona. Her teeth were chattering from the freezing water. Her lips were blue. But she smiled back at me.

And I felt awesome.

17

BACK
FROM
BEYOND

Frank Goolz took the Hand of Chaos, the magic mirror, and the live slug from the jar from the Farrells' lab, and stored them in his library of paranormal artifacts. Uncle Jerry left us to go back to hunting hairier, not-so-slimy creatures in the cold wilderness up north. He was bitterly disappointed that Frank Goolz wouldn't give him either the slug or the horn so he could engineer more monsters.

"I guess you earned the Mallow Marsh Monster," he said sadly, getting into his beat-up station wagon. "If you ever want to create a new monster and get richer than the Queen, call me!" He mimed a telephone with his hand, waved, and winked at us as he drove away.

Thanks to the Sleep-o-Stick and our increasing

ability to conceal our adventures, Mum stayed unaware of the grave danger I had been through to save the Farrells. Now that she believed we all played according to her rules, she stopped using so many expletives when she talked about the Goolz. I often caught her standing by our kitchen window smiling when she saw Frank Goolz come out of his house to sit on his porch swing with a cup of coffee in his hand. Sometimes, she would join him with her cup of tea, and they would talk about parenthood in general and us, their wonderful kids, in particular. At least that's what I assumed they talked about.

. . .

I was by my window, looking at the Goolz's home and waiting for Ilona to join me for a homework session when someone knocked on the front door. I dropped my tablet on the bed and rushed to the hallway as Mum answered the door. I slowed when I saw that it wasn't Ilona.

It was the Farrell twins and the woman I had known as the Mallow Marsh Monster—the very creature that I had stabbed with a syringe in the marsh.

Mrs. Farrell looked better than ever. She wore a long, white linen shirt with jeans and pounds of jade and turquoise necklaces. She was smiling warmly and looked much younger than I remembered her from before her monster days. She looked like an angel—but maybe it was just the contrast with her greener self that made me think so.

"Oh, Harold," Mum said when she saw me at the top of the stairs. "Your new friends wanted to see you. Won't you come down and say hi?"

"Won't I, indeed!" I said, mimicking Mum's British accent, which got stronger when she was nervous.

I slid into the stair lift, held tight to my wheelchair, and pressed the button to go down. The Farrell twins were fascinated by the process, staring at me like I had just reinvented fire.

"Is it fun?"

"It looks fun—"

"Going down like that."

"Ha!"

"Well, hello, Harold," Mrs. Farrell said when I joined them by the door.

"Hello." I stopped at a safe distance. I still felt a tinge of fear, despite her smile and kind voice.

She came to me and shook my hand. "I wanted to thank you personally, Harold. You're a very brave boy."

"Oh, that's nice," Mum said awkwardly. "But . . . thank him for what, exactly?"

I shook my head, hoping none of the Farrells would tell our story.

"Why are you shaking your head, Harold?" Mum asked, picking up on the strange vibe. "Is there something I should know?"

Mrs. Farrell smiled at her. "Nothing special," she said, catching on. "I just wanted to thank him for being such a good friend to my daughters. They didn't know anybody in town and Harold has been . . . exceptional."

"I see." Mum beamed at the compliment. "He's a lovely boy," she agreed and invited everybody in for tea and cookies.

"That would be wonderful," Mrs. Farrell said and we all went to sit at the kitchen table. Mum brought the twins and me tall glasses of milk and made tea for herself and Mrs. Farrell. She put a plate of her homemade cookies in the middle of the table. Mrs. Farrell immediately grabbed one and put it in her mouth whole. I looked at her suspiciously.

She swallowed the cookie with a gulp of tea. "I'm sorry. I have been just ravenous lately."

"Oh, that's fine," Mum said brightly, though she looked surprised by Mrs. Farrell's unusual table manners. "There are plenty more cookies."

I took one. The twins took one each. Mrs. Farrell

took a second and a third and the plate was empty.

"I'm afraid I'm a little confused," Mum said, rising to get the cookie tin from the counter. "I didn't know Harold and your daughters had become friends."

"We see each other around." I shrugged. "Nothing wrong with that."

"We met at the Goolz's."

"Didn't he tell you?"

"All the strange things."

"Unusual."

"Bizarre—"

"That happened—"

"There!" They pointed at the Goolz's home.

Mum looked at me strangely, but thankfully her phone buzzed from the kitchen counter before she could ask any questions. She answered and went out to the porch to talk to one of her clients.

"She doesn't know anything about the monster," I whispered to the Farrells. "Not a thing. So zip it about that." I looked pointedly at the twins and they nodded as one.

"I gathered that," Mrs. Farrell said. "Don't worry. We won't say a word. Right, girls?"

Both twins shrugged and drank up their milk, gulping it at the exact same speed.

"You saved our mom," they said, wiping their milk mustaches with the back of their hands.

"She says that if it weren't for you—"

"We would all be monsters."

"She says you're like a superhero."

"She talks about you."

"*All. The. Time!*"

"Okay," I agreed hesitantly. I didn't see myself as a superhero, but it felt great to hear it.

I wiped off my own milk mustache. "When I was transforming, were you . . . inside my head?"

"Yes. I could feel, hear, sense everything that you did. There were quite a lot of amazing perks being a monster."

"Really? Like, you enjoyed it? Being a monster?" I asked Mrs. Farrell. "I was dead scared when I was changing into one."

She chewed her third cookie thoughtfully. "Well, I was scared too, Harold. In the beginning. But once you've fully turned, you feel . . ." she searched for the right word, "wonderful."

We drank our tea and milk silently, ruminating on the perks of being a monster.

"There's another thing I really need to ask you," I said. "What did you do to Ms. Pincher's dog?"

"Well." Mrs. Farrell blushed. "I'm afraid I devoured it. It was delicious. At the time, that is." She washed down the last of her cookie with the rest of her tea while the twins giggled.

Mum came back, and the twins and I left them alone and went to see the Goolz.

"There's your girlfriend," the twins said, pointing.

Ilona came across the little bridge. She didn't seem surprised to see that the twins were with me. It seemed they'd gained membership to our little club of misfits.

"Where's your sister?"

"She's nice."

"And fun."

"And she likes us."

"She's inside," Ilona told them. "Playing with Dad's new toy."

"New toy?" I repeated.

"It's awesome. You want to come see it?"

The twins were as excited as I was, but they didn't know that a toy for Frank Goolz meant something like a demonic Rubik's Cube or booby trap for a ghost.

"You're going to love this, Harold!" Suzie shouted when we went inside. She wore a semitransparent beanie that smelled like old rubber and was connected to a network of electrical cables.

"Hello," the twins said, waving at Suzie.

"Oh. You," Suzie said, losing a bit of her enthusiasm. "You didn't bring another body part, did you?"

"No," they said, touching the cables connected to Suzie's hat.

"What is that?" I asked, approaching her.

Frank Goolz bounded into the room. "*That*, Harold, is a dream machine, obviously!" He knelt and started screwing the ends of the cables to a metal box. I maneuvered around the cords to get a closer look.

"That's the new toy?" I asked.

"This is anything but a toy." Frank Goolz stood up, dropping his screwdriver, which bounced off the box with a loud bang.

"It looks old," I said, noticing the patches of rust on the sides.

Frank Goolz carelessly kicked it with his bare foot. "It is old. And it's the only one of its kind." Frank Goolz flicked a switch on the box and the machine started to hum loudly.

"Can we try the funny hat?"

"Do you have two?"

"We need to do it at the same time."

"Together."

"As one."

"*Always!*"

"No!" Suzie took a step away. "There's only one hat. And it's mine!"

"It isn't yours," Ilona said. "You have to share."

"Of course." Frank Goolz turned the last switch. "Everyone will try it. It's harmless."

"What does it do?" I asked. The humming had gotten even louder and I had to raise my voice.

"It controls dreams by interacting electrically with the brain." Frank Goolz touched a large red button in the middle of the box. "If I press this button and adjust these levels," he tapped a series of dials along the side of the box, "I could force Suzie to dream whatever I want."

"A dream machine," I mused. "That sounds like fun."

"Press the button, Dad!" Suzie said, holding the beanie tight against her head.

"Well, I don't see why not." Frank Goolz hovered his hand over the red button. The machine seemed to anticipate his touch and began humming at a painfully high pitch.

"Here goes," Frank Goolz said. He pressed the red button, and *POP!*

All hell broke loose.

ACKNOWLEDGMENTS

Thanks to Dulce and Ruben Gerson for their loving and steady support, to Maria Ahlund for being my partner in crime, to Jacques and Sylvie Flatin for their friendship, to Isabelle Perrin for being such an amazing creative force behind the Goolz series, to Bernard Cros for enduring all of our silliness, and to Valentin and Tim Cros for being our devoted test readers.

Thanks to Morgane Dupay for taking care of the essential.

Thanks to Thomas Leclere for all his work and for being an indefatigable champion for everything Goolz, and to his team at Le Seuil Jeunesse—Olivia Godat, Aude Marin, and everyone else—you know who you are!

Thanks to Trish and Franco for being my very good friends, and to Franco for being the real-life inspiration for the amazing Uncle Jerry in this installment of the Goolz's adventures.

Thanks to my agent extraordinaire, Alexa Stark at Trident Media Group, for all her work and support for this project.

And special thanks to my editor Mary Colgan—and all her colleagues who helped us greatly improve this novel with their own talent and commitment—Liz Van Doren, Brittany Ryan, Suzy Krogulski, and Toni Willis. Mary, this is our ten-year anniversary working together on funny/scary novels. We are definitely due for a cake and a few candles.

Born in Paris to an international family (one part French, two parts Spanish, one part strange), Gary Ghislain grew up between Paris and the French Riviera. He now lives in Antibes with his two daughters, Ilo and Sisko. He is also the author of Harold and the Goolz's first adventure, *A Bad Night for Bullies*. Visit him at garyghislain.blogspot.com.